"Want help with that g... cowboy said as he brushed against her.

"Thank you." Dulcie ducked out from under his arms and stood back to watch him drag it out of the way. He wasn't just tall, she realized. His shoulder muscles bunched, stretching the fabric of his Western shirt across broad shoulders. And as he opened the gate, she got a good look at his body.

"Mind if I ask what you're planning to do here?" He gestured toward the house.

"Having a look around."

He leaned against the gatepost, studying her. "I hadn't taken you for one of them."

"I beg your pardon?"

"The morbidly curious."

Dulcie felt something in her tense. "I'm afraid I don't know what you're talking about."

"Don't you? A woman was murdered in that house."

Dear Harlequin Intrigue Reader,

We hope you enjoy *Smokin' Six-Shooter* written by *USA TODAY* bestselling author B.J. Daniels.

Harlequin Intrigue is the ultimate romance suspense series. If you love following trace evidence and tracking down leads right along with lawmen and investigators, we have a terrific lineup of six can't-put-down stories available every month.

Join us at Harlequin Intrigue as we crack the hardest cases and unravel the deepest mysteries of the heart.

Happy reading,

The Harlequin Intrigue Editors

P.S. Visit www.tryharlequin.com to download over 16 free books and experience the variety of romances that we publish!

B.J. DANIELS

SMOKIN' SIX-SHOOTER

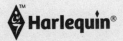

TORONTO NEW YORK LONDON
AMSTERDAM PARIS SYDNEY HAMBURG
STOCKHOLM ATHENS TOKYO MILAN MADRID
PRAGUE WARSAW BUDAPEST AUCKLAND

Copyright © 2011 by Harlequin Books S.A.

ISBN-13: 978-0-373-20276-8

The contents of this book may have been
edited from their original format. The publisher
acknowledges the copyright holders of the
individual works as follows:

SMOKIN' SIX-SHOOTER
Copyright © 2009 by Barbara Heinlein

Excerpt from GI COWBOY
Copyright © 2011 by Delores Fossen

ABOUT THE AUTHOR

USA TODAY bestselling author **B.J. Daniels** began writing novels after a career as a newspaper journalist. The author of more than fifty titles for Harlequin Books, she has won numerous awards, including a career achievement award for romantic suspense. Her books regularly appear on bestseller lists.

B.J. lives in Montana with her husband and their two springer spaniels. When she isn't plotting her next book, she snowboards, camps, boats and plays tennis. She is a member of the Mystery Writers of America, Sisters in Crime, Thriller Writers, Kiss of Death and Romance Writers of America.

Visit her website at www.bjdaniels.com or email her at bjdaniels@mtintouch.net.

Look for B.J. Daniels's next books from Harlequin Intrigue!

#1276 BRANDED
Whitehorse, Montana: Chisholm Cattle Company
May 2011

#1282 LASSOED
Whitehorse, Montana: Chisholm Cattle Company
June 2011

#1288 RUSTLED
Whitehorse, Montana: Chisholm Cattle Company
July 2011

#1294 STAMPEDED
Whitehorse, Montana: Chisholm Cattle Company
August 2011

CAST OF CHARACTERS

Russell Corbett—He feared city girl Dulcie Hughes was in over her head. He had no idea just how deep.

Dulcie Hughes—She'd come to Montana to solve the mystery of her inheritance, only to find a killer.

Laura Beaumont—She'd left behind more than just her property. There was her unsolved murder.

Jolene Stevens—Someone was writing a short story about a real unsolved murder and leaving them for the new teacher at the one-room schoolhouse.

Tinker Horton—The rodeo cowboy had a standing date with the teacher when he was in town. It seemed the perfect relationship for both of them.

Finnegan Amherst—Had the rainmaker come back after twenty-four years to make rain? Or tie up some loose ends?

Ben Carpenter—The local ranch manager had known the dead woman, but how well?

Ronda Carpenter—The tiny, mousy woman seemed to live in fear. Was her fear for her son Tinker from another marriage? Or was it for the son she'd had with Ben?

Midge Atkinson—The matronly woman had almost lost her husband to Laura Beaumont. It wasn't something she'd soon forget.

John Atkinson—He'd lost the woman of his dreams and was paying for it.

Chapter One

"There must be some mistake." Dulcie Hughes shifted in her chair, anxious to flee the lawyer's office. "We've covered everything my parents left me in their estate."

"Not this particular part of your inheritance," he said and cleared this throat. For years Lawrence Brooks Sr. had been her parents' attorney, but upon his death his youngest son, Herbert, had taken over his father's law practice.

Herbert was in his early thirties, only a few years older than Dulcie herself, a tall, prematurely balding man with tiny brown eyes and a nervous twitch.

Today though he seemed even more nervous than usual, which made her pay closer attention as he handed her the documents.

"What is this?" she asked, frowning. Her elderly parents had discussed all their financial arrangements with her at length for years. She'd never seen this before.

"You've been left some property in Montana."

"*Montana?*"

He tried to still his hands as he waited for her to read the documents.

"My parents never mentioned anything about having property in Montana." She read the name. "Who is Laura Beaumont?"

"You don't know?"

She shook her head. "I've never heard the name before. This is all the information you have?"

"Apparently Laura Beaumont's estate was being held for you in a trust until their deaths, taking care of the expenses. That's all I can tell you." He stood abruptly, signaling an end to their business.

Dulcie didn't move. "Are you saying this is all you *know* or this is all you're *allowed* to tell me?"

"If you want to know more, I would suggest you obtain an attorney of your own to look into the matter further," he said, tapping his fingertips on his desk as he waited impatiently for her to leave. "Or go to Montana yourself." He made the latter sound imprudent.

"Maybe I'll do that," Dulcie said, rising to her feet and tucking the papers into her shoulder bag.

"As your parents' attorney, that completes our business," Herbert said, sounding glad of it.

For the past four months, she'd been grieving the loss of her parents and not in the least interested in dealing with the financial aspects of that loss.

As the only heir of Brad and Kathy Hughes, she'd known she would be inheriting a sizable estate. Not that she needed it. Straight out of college, she and a friend had opened a boutique that had taken off.

After establishing more than a dozen such shops across the country, she and Renada had sold the businesses six months ago and made enough that she would never have to work again if she invested the money wisely, which of course she had.

She'd been trying to decide what to do next when her seventy-two-year-old father had taken ill. Her mother had never been strong, suffering from a weak heart.

But to lose both of them within a few weeks had been crushing.

Now, months later, she felt even more at loose ends.

As she left the lawyer's office, her cell phone rang.

"So it's over?" asked her friend and former business partner tentatively. Renada had wanted to come along with her to see the lawyer, knowing how hard this was for her. But Dulcie had needed to do this on her own. She needed to get used to doing a lot of things on her own.

"All done," she said, patting the papers she'd stuffed into her shoulder bag.

"Up for lunch?" Renada asked.

"Absolutely. I'm starved." And she was, she realized.

It wasn't until after they'd eaten and she was feeling better for the first time in months that she told her friend about the Montana property.

"It's very odd," she said, digging out the papers the lawyer had given her. "I've been left property in Montana from someone named Laura Beaumont."

"Seriously? How much?"

"Apparently a hundred and sixty acres just outside of Whitehorse, Montana."

"Where is that?"

"I haven't a clue."

"Aren't you curious about this Laura Beaumont?"

"Yes, but it's so strange that my parents never mentioned this woman or anything about the property, even though Laura Beaumont left it to me years ago."

"Your parents never even went to Montana to see what you'd been left?"

"Apparently not. We went to Yellowstone Park one summer. Wouldn't you think they'd have mentioned the property?"

"Or taken you there. Unless it's in the middle of nowhere and they had no interest in it. You are going to check it out, aren't you?"

Dulcie knew her friend had been worried about her, urging her to come up with another business venture to help get her through her loss. "Do you want to go with me?"

Renada shook her head ruefully. "I'd love to, but I can't leave right now. I just agreed to teach some clothing-design classes at the community university."

"Good for you," Dulcie said, excited for her friend. Renada had always talked about doing something like this when she had the time. Their boutiques had kept them so busy she'd never gotten the chance. Now there was nothing keeping her from it.

"It's funny," Dulcie said as they walked out of the restaurant together. "I got the feeling from the lawyer that there was something unusual about this inheritance."

"Unusual how?"

"Something he couldn't talk about. Or wouldn't."

"A *secret?*" Renada said on an excited breath. "Maybe this land is worth a small fortune. Or Lewis and Clark left their names carved in the stones on the property."

Dulcie laughed. "Don't get your hopes up. I'm sure it's just a piece of property that is so inconsequential that it skipped my parents' minds."

"A hundred and sixty acres in Montana inconsequential?" Renada scoffed. "Still, it *does* seem odd since you've never heard of this Laura Beaumont. So when are you going to Montana?"

"Right away, I guess," Dulcie said, feeling as if this was a decision that had been taken out of her hands a long time ago.

* * *

*A HOT, DRY WIND WHISPERED in the curtains as the
weather vane on the barn turned restlessly, groaning
and creaking.*

*The air in the house was so hot it hurt to breathe.
The parched land outside the old farmhouse with its
ochre dried grasses seemed to ache for a drink in the
undulating heat waves that moved across the prairie as
far as the eye could see.*

*Like the land, she'd forgotten the smell of rain, the
feel of it soaking into her skin. She thirsted for the sound
of raindrops on the roof, the splash of mud puddles as
a pickup drove past.*

*She lay naked on the bed in the upstairs bedroom, the
hot wind moving over her lush body, leaving it glistening
with perspiration. Too young and ripe to be widowed,
she ached for more than a cool breeze to caress her
flesh.*

*The noise of the whirling fan across the room cov-
ered the creak of the slow, deliberate footsteps on the
stairs. While she didn't hear anyone, she must have felt
a change in the air that told her she was no longer alone
in the house.*

*"Is that you, sweetie?" she asked without expending
the energy it would take to open her eyes. "I thought
you'd gone down to the creek with your little friend."*

No answer.

*A chill skittered over her, dimpling her flawless skin.
Her eyes flew open in alarm as if she heard the blade
cutting through the oppressive heat.*

*The first stab of the knife stole her breath. She tried
to sit up, but the next blow knocked her back. The at-
tacks came more quickly now, metal to flesh to bone,*

burning deep as blood pooled on the clean white sheets, the blood as hot as the breathless air around her.

By the time the knife finally stilled, its wielder panting hard from the exertion in the close heat of that second-story bedroom, she lay with her head turned toward the door, eyes dull with death, the face of her killer reflected accusingly in her dark pupils.

JOLENE STEVENS DROPPED the neatly printed pages and let out the breath she'd been holding. She glanced past the glow of her desk lamp to the door of the Old Town Whitehorse one-room schoolhouse.

The door was open to let in what cool night air might be had this late spring day. Like the beginning of the story she'd just read, the heat had been intense for weeks now. There wasn't a breath of cool air and little chance of rain, according to the weatherman.

Jolene fanned herself with her grade book as she looked down at the pages again. On Friday she'd given her students an assignment to begin a short fictional story that would be told in six segments. She'd told them they didn't have to put their names on their stories, thinking this would make them less self-conscious.

Each story was typed, double-spaced, on the student's home computer so all of the stories looked the same.

While she'd instructed her students to start their stories at an exciting part and introduce an interesting character or intriguing place or event, she hadn't expected anything this disturbing.

Mentally, she envisioned each of her five students: Amy Brooks, the precocious third-grade girl; the two goof-off fifth-grade boys, Thad Brooks and Luke Raines; the sixth-grade cowgirl, Codi Fox, and the eighth-grade moody boy on the cusp of becoming a man, Mace Carpenter.

She couldn't imagine any of them writing this. Picking up the assignments, she counted. *Six?* Five students and yet she had collected *six* short-story beginnings? Was it possible one of them had turned in two stories?

For the first time since Jolene had come to Old Town Whitehorse to teach in the one-room schoolhouse, she felt uneasy. She'd been hired right out of Montana State University to fill an opening when the former teacher ran off and got married just before the school year ended, so all of this was new to her.

She rose and walked to the door to look out. Night sounds carried on the breeze. Crickets chirped in the tall dried grass of the empty lot between the school and the Whitehorse Community Center. No other sound could be heard in the hot Monday night since little remained of the town except for a few old buildings.

Her bike still leaned against the front of the school where she'd left it. Past it she could make out the playground equipment hunkered in the dark inside the old iron fence.

Beyond the playground, the arch over the cemetery on the hill seemed to catch some moonlight. She'd been warned about strange lights in the cemetery late at night. Talk was that the place was haunted.

Jolene had loved the idea, loved everything about this quaint rural community and her first teaching job. She loved the rolling prairie and even the isolation. She was shy, an avid reader, and appreciated the peace and quiet that the near-ghost town of Old Town Whitehorse afforded.

But the short-story beginning had left her on edge. She shivered even though the night was unbearably hot. Nothing moved in the darkness outside the schoolhouse.

The only light was one of those large yard lights used on ranches, shining from down the road by the small house that came with her teaching position.

Jolene closed the door, locking it, and stood for a moment studying the tables and chairs where her students sat. Light pooled on her desk, illuminating the rest of the opening scenes waiting there for her to read.

Tomorrow her students would turn in their next segment of their short stories, the assignment to run for another five days, ending next Monday. Would there be more of this story?

Earlier she had decided to stay late and read the first of the stories here where she'd thought it might be cooler. Now, with the murder story too fresh in her mind, she changed her mind and, stepping to the desk, scooped up the assignments and shoved them into her backpack.

An owl hooted just outside the open window, making her jump. She laughed at her own foolishness. She'd been raised in the country, and having been a tomboy, nothing had scared her. So why was she letting some fictional tale scare her?

Because she couldn't believe that any of her students had written it, she thought, as she zipped her backpack shut and turned out the lamp. She moved through the dark schoolroom to the door, unlocked it and stepped out.

The heat hit her like a fist and for a moment, she had trouble catching her breath. The weather this spring was *too* much like the short story, she thought, as she climbed on her bike and rode down the hill to her small house.

Once inside, she turned on all the lights, feeling foolish. What was there to be frightened of in this nearly deserted town in the middle of nowhere? The murder in the story had just been someone's vivid imagination at work. Vivid, *gruesome* imagination at work.

She made herself a sandwich and sat down with the rest of the stories. They were all pretty much what she'd expected from each of her students and she'd easily recognized each student's work.

Just as she'd suspected—none of them had written the brutal murder story. But one of them had to have turned it in. Why?

The answer seemed obvious.

Someone wanted her to read it.

Chapter Two

Dulcie Hughes brought the rented car to a stop in front of a boarded-up old farmhouse in the middle of nowhere.

This was it? The mysterious Montana property? She couldn't help her disappointment. She hadn't known what to expect when she'd flown into Great Falls and driven across what was called the Hi-Line to Whitehorse.

The small Western town hadn't been much of a surprise, either, after driving through one small Western town after another.

She had driven under the train tracks into Whitehorse, telling herself she understood why her parents had never brought her here. There wasn't much to see unless you liked cowboys and pickup trucks. That seemed to be the only thing along the main street.

A few bars, churches, cafés and a couple of clothing stores later, she had to backtrack to find a real-estate office for directions to her property.

A cute blonde named April had drawn her a map and told her she couldn't miss it. Of course that wasn't true given that the land and all the old farmhouses looked alike. Fortunately she had the GPS coordinates.

The difference also was that her farmhouse had apparently been boarded up for years. Weeds had grown tall behind the barbed-wire fence. Nothing about the house looked in the least bit inviting.

"How do you feel about bats?" April had asked.

"*Bats?*"

"Whitehorse is the northernmost range for migrating little brown bats. They hibernate down in the Little Rockies and Memorial Day they show up in Whitehorse and don't leave till after Labor Day. They come for the mosquitoes. I hope someone warned you about the mosquitoes. And the wind."

"Don't worry, I won't be staying long. I've just come to see the property for myself before I put it on the market."

"So you don't think you'll be falling in love with it up here and never want to leave?" April joked.

Dulcie wondered all the way across the top of the state why anyone in their right mind lived here.

"I thought there would be mountains and pine trees," she had said to April.

"The Little Rockies are forty miles to the south. There's pine trees down there. Ponderosas. Your property isn't far from there." She'd grinned. "I guess you missed the single pine tree on the edge of town and the sign somebody put up that reads, Whitehorse County National Forest."

Funny. But stuff like that was probably all they had to do around here for fun, Dulcie had thought as she had taken the map and thanked April for her help, promising to get back to her about listing the property.

For Dulcie, who lived in Chicago, the pine trees and the mountains had been farther than she thought—about twenty miles away.

She grabbed her cell phone, unable to wait a moment longer to call Renada and give her the news. But as she flipped it open, she heard the roar of an engine and looked into her rearview mirror to find a huge farm machine of some kind barreling down on her.

Fumbling for the key in the ignition, she let out a cry and braced herself for the inevitable crash as her rental car was suddenly shrouded in a cloud of dust.

She must have closed her eyes, waiting for the impact, because when she opened them, she found a pair of very blue, very angry eyes scowling in at her.

Turning the key, she whirred down her window since the cowboy hunkered next to her rental car seemed to be mouthing something.

"Yes?" she inquired, cell phone still in hand in case she needed to call for help. "Is there a problem?"

He quirked a brow. "Other than you parked in the middle of the road just over a rise? Nope, that about covers it."

"I'm sorry. Let me pull off the road so you can get around."

"Going to take more than that to get a combine through here on this narrow stretch of road, I'm afraid."

A combine. How interesting.

"You lost?" he asked, shoving back his battered gray Stetson to glance over the top of her rental toward the farmhouse, then back to her.

He had the most direct blue-eyed stare she'd ever seen.

"No." Not that it was any of his business. "I think I've seen all I need to see here so I'll just go on up the road."

"The road dead-ends a mile in the direction you're headed," he said. "But if that's what you want to do. I'm only going another half mile. I can follow you."

Oh, wouldn't that be delightful.

"I believe in that case I'll just pull into this house and let you go by," she said and started to open her door.

"Want help with the gate?" he asked with a hint of amusement as he stepped back to let her slide from the car.

"I'm sure I can figure it out." She straightened to her full height of five-nine, counting the two-inch heels of her dress boots, but he still towered over her.

Turning her back to him, she walked to the barbed-wire gate strung across the road into the house. She could feel his gaze appraising her and wished she'd worn something more appropriate.

Renada had joked that she needed to buy herself a pair of cowboy boots. She had worn designer jeans, a blouse and a pair of black dress boots with heels. As one of her heels sank into the soft dirt, she wished she'd taken Renada's advice.

The gate, she found, had an odd contraption at one end, with a wire from the fence post that looped over the gatepost. Apparently all she had to do to open the gate was slip the wire loop off that post.

The gate, though, hadn't been opened in a while, judging from how deep the wire had sunk into the old wood. The wire dug into her fingers as she tried to slide it upward.

"You have to hug it," the cowboy said, brushing against her as he leaned over her to wrap one arm around the gatepost and the other around the fence post and squeezed. As the two posts came together, he easily slid the wire loop up and off.

"Thank you," she said as she ducked out from under his arms and stood back to watch him drag the gate out of the way. He wasn't just tall, she realized. His shoulder muscles bunched as he opened the gate, stretching the fabric of his Western shirt across his broad shoulders, and she'd gotten a good look at his backside.

The only cowboys she'd seen in Chicago were the urban types. None of them had this man's rough-and-tough appearance. Nor had their jeans fit them quite like this cowboy's did, she couldn't help noticing.

"I'd be watching out for rattlesnakes if I were you," he called after her as she turned to head for her car.

He's just trying to scare me, she told herself but made a point of walking slowly back to her rental car and hurriedly getting inside—much to his amusement.

She revved the engine and pulled into the yard of her property, glad when she would be seeing the last of him. As she did, something moved behind a missing shutter at an upstairs window.

"Just leave the gate," Dulcie said, cutting the engine and getting out of the car. "I might as well have a look around while I'm here."

He leaned against the gatepost studying her. "Excuse me for saying so, but I don't think that's a good idea. I wasn't joking about the rattlers, especially around an old place like this. Not to mention the fact that you're trespassing and people around here don't take kindly to that. You could get yourself shot."

This last part she really doubted. "I'll take my chances."

He shrugged. "I hadn't taken you for one of them."

"I beg your pardon?"

"The morbidly curious."

Dulcie felt something in her tense. "I'm afraid I don't know what you're talking about."

"A woman was murdered in that house."

She shook her head, not trusting her voice.

"Change your mind about hanging out here?"

"No." The word came out weakly.

He tried to hide a grin. "Then I should probably warn you that if you get into trouble that cell phone you've been clutching won't be of any use. There's no coverage out here."

She lifted an eyebrow. She'd never had trouble getting coverage with her cell phone carrier. The man didn't know what he was talking about. She snapped open her phone. Damn, he was right.

When she looked up he was walking back toward his combine, shaking his head with each long stride. She could hear him muttering under his breath. "Got better things to do than stand around in this heat arguing with some fool city girl who doesn't have the sense God gave her."

"So much for Western hospitality," she muttered under her own breath, then turned toward the house and felt herself shiver despite the heat.

JOLENE STEVENS GLANCED at the clock on the schoolhouse wall. The hot air coming through the open windows and the sound of the birds and crickets chirping in the grass had all five students looking wistfully toward the cloudless blue sky and the summerlike day outside.

"Hand in your writing assignments and you may go home a few minutes early," she said, giving up the fight to keep their attention. "Don't forget you have another part of your story to write tonight. Tomorrow we will talk about writing the middle of your story."

The air was close inside the schoolhouse, the breeze coming through the open window as hot as dragon's breath against the back of her neck.

Jolene lifted her hair as she waited for her sixth-grader, Codi Fox, to collect all the assignments. She tried not to let any of her students see how anxious she was, not that they were paying attention. As Codi put the stack of short stories on the corner of her desk, Jolene made a point of not looking at them.

Instead she watched as her students pulled on their backpacks, answered questions and wished everyone a nice evening. None of them seemed in the least bit interested in the short-story assignments they'd just turned in.

If one of the students was bringing her the extra story, wouldn't he or she have been anxious to see Jolene's reaction? Apparently not.

After they'd all left, she straightened chairs, turned out lights, picked up around the schoolroom. The small, snub-nosed school bus came and went, taking three of her students with it. She waved to the elderly woman driver, then stood in the shade of the doorway as the parents of her last two students pulled up.

As soon as the dust settled, Jolene went back inside the classroom to her desk. Her hands were actually trembling as she picked up the short-story assignments, afraid the next installment of the murder story would be among the pile—and afraid it wouldn't.

She quickly counted the individual stories. *Six.*

With a sigh of relief and an air of apprehension, she sorted through until she found it.

IT HAD BEEN ONE THOSE HOT, *dry springs when all the churchgoers in Whitehorse County were praying for rain. The small farming community depended on spring rains and when they didn't come, you could feel the anxiety growing like a low-frequency electrical pulse that raced through the county and left everyone on edge.*

Everyone, that is, but her. She wasn't worried that day about the weather as she hung her wet sheets on the line behind the old farmhouse and waited—not for rain but for the sound of his truck coming up the dead-end road.

JOLENE SWALLOWED AND looked up, afraid someone would come through the school's door at any minute and catch her. Reading this felt like a guilty pleasure. Gathering up her work, she stuffed everything into her backpack and biked home.

Once there, she poured herself a glass of lemonade and, unable to postpone it any longer, picked up the story again.

THE SWELTERING HEAT ON THE wind wrapped her long skirt around her slim legs, and lifted her mane of dark hair off her damp neck as she stared past the clothesline to the dirt road, anticipating her lover's arrival.

She'd sent the little girl off to play with her new friend from across the creek. A long, lazy afternoon stretched endlessly before her and she ached at the thought, her need to be fulfilled by a man as essential as her next breath.

Over the sound of the weather vane on the barn groaning in the wind and the snap of the sheets as she secured them to the line, she finally heard a vehicle.

Her head came up and softened with relief, a clothespin between her perfect white teeth, her lightly freckled arms clutching the line as if for support as she watched him turn into the yard.

Dust roiled up into the blindingly bright day, the scorching wind lifting and carrying it across the road to the empty prairie.

She took the clothespin from her mouth, licking her lips as she secured the sheet, then leaving the rest of her wet clothes in the basket, she wiped her hands on her skirt and hurried to meet the man who would be the death of her.

JOLENE TOOK A BREATH and then reread the pages. She had no more clue as to who could have written this than she had the first time. Nor was she sure why the submission upset her the way it did. It was just fiction, right?

Why give it to her to read though? All she could think was that one of her student's parents always wanted to write and was looking for some encouragement.

"All my daughter talks about is the short story you're having the students write," Amy's mother had told her. "The other students and their families are talking about it, as well. You've excited the whole community since I'm told the stories will eventually be bound in a booklet that will be for sale at next year's fall festival."

Was that how the author of the murder story had found out about the assignment? Which meant it could be anyone, not necessarily one of her student's parents. But one of the students had to be bringing it in to class.

Jolene got up and went to the window, hoping for a breath of fresh air. Heat rose in waves over the pale yellow wild grass that ran to the Little Rockies.

What did the writer expect her to do with this? Just read it? Critique it? Believe it?

She shuddered as she realized that from the first sentence she'd read of the story, she *had* believed it. But then that was what good fiction was all about, making the reader suspend disbelief.

Even though she knew how the story ended since

the writer had begun with the murder, she had the feeling that the writer was far from finished. At least she hoped that was the case. She couldn't bear the thought that whoever was sending her this might just quit in the middle and leave her hanging.

She looked forward to seeing the next part of the story Wednesday morning and didn't want to think that she might never know who or why someone had given it to her to read. As disturbing as the story was, she felt flattered that the writer had chosen her to read it.

As she stood looking out the window, she had a thought. Had such a murder occurred in this community? The old-timers around here told stories back to the first settlers. If there *had* been a brutal murder around here, she was sure someone would be able to recall it.

Especially one involving a young widow with a daughter living in an old farmhouse one very hot, rainless spring.

Jolene glanced back up the road to the Whitehorse Community Center. Several pickups and an SUV were parked out front for the meeting of the Whitehorse Sewing Circle. If anyone knew about a murder, it would be one of those women.

DULCIE WAITED UNTIL THE dust settled from the combine and the cowboy before she turned back to the house. Her gaze was drawn to the second-floor window again and the pale yellow curtain.

She was sure the color had faded over the years and she couldn't make out the design on the fabric from here, but something about that yellow curtain felt oddly familiar.

Careful to make sure no rattlesnakes had snuck up while she'd been waiting, she took a few tentative steps toward the house. Had she seen this house with its yellow curtains in a photograph? Surely her parents had one somewhere.

Boards had been nailed across the front door and the lower windows. There would be no getting into the house without some tools. But did she really want to go inside?

She noticed a sliver of window visible from beneath the boards and moved cautiously through the tall weeds to cup her hands and peer inside.

She blinked in surprise. The inside of the house was covered in dust, but it looked as if whoever had lived here had just walked out one day and not returned.

The furniture appeared to be right where it had been, including a book on a side table and a drinking glass, now filled with cobwebs and dust, where someone had sat and read. There were tracks where small critters had obviously made themselves at home, but other than that, the place looked as if it hadn't been disturbed in years.

Since the murder?

Dulcie felt a chill and told herself the cowboy might have just made that up to scare her, the same way he had warned her about rattlesnakes.

According to the documents, Dulcie had been left the property twenty-four years before. She would have been four.

Who left property to a four-year-old?

Laura Beaumont apparently.

Dulcie drew back, brushed dust from her sleeve and started to turn to the rental car to leave when she heard a strange creaking groan that made her freeze.

What sent her pulse soaring was the realization that she'd heard this exact sound before. She found her feet and stepped around the side of the house to look in the direction the noise was coming from.

On top of the barn, a rusted weather vane in the shape of a horse moved in the breeze, groaning and creaking restlessly.

Dulcie stood staring at it, her eyes suddenly welling with tears. She *had* been here before. The thought filled her with a horrible sense of dread.

She wiped at the tears, convinced she was losing her mind. Why else did a pair of yellow curtains and a rusted weather vane make her feel such dread—and worse—such fear?

Chapter Three

Russell Corbett drove the combine down the road to where he'd left his four-wheeler. He hated trading the luxury of the cab of the combine with its CD player, satellite radio and air conditioner for the noisy, hot four-wheeler.

He much preferred a horse to a vehicle anyway, but he couldn't argue the convenience as he started the engine and headed back toward Trails West Ranch.

As he neared the old Beaumont place, it was impossible not to think about the woman he'd almost crashed into earlier, sitting in the middle of the road. Fool city girl, he thought, shaking his head again. Thinking about her took his mind off the heat bearing down on him.

He hadn't paid that much attention to her. Even now he couldn't recall her exact hair color. Something between russet and mahogany, but then it had been hard to tell with the sunlight firing it with gold.

Nor could he recall the length, the way she had the weight of her hair drawn up and secured in the back. He idly wondered if it would fall past her shoulders should the expensive-looking clip come loose.

He did remember her size when he'd bent over her, no more than five-six or seven without those heels, and recalled the impression he'd gotten that while her body was slim, she was rounded in all the right places. He'd sensed a strength about her, or maybe it had just been mule-headed stubbornness, that belied her stature and her obvious city-girl background.

Realizing the path his thoughts had taken, Russell shook them off like water from a wet dog. He must be suffering from heatstroke, he told himself. No woman had monopolized his thoughts this long in recent memory.

He told himself he wasn't even going to look as he passed to see if she was still parked in front of the old farmhouse as he passed. It was too hot to save her from herself, even if she had wanted his help.

But he did look and told himself it wasn't disappointment he felt at finding her gone. It was relief that she wasn't in some trouble he would have to get her out of.

He slowed the four-wheeler as he noticed the fence lying on the ground. With a curse, he stopped and got off to close it. The woman had a lot to learn about private property and leaving gates open, he thought.

Glancing at the house, he was glad to see that nothing looked any different. Not that the woman could do much damage to the place. No way could she have broken into the house—not with those manicured fingernails of hers.

He'd never paid much attention to the old Beaumont place, although he'd passed it enough times since the land just beyond it was Corbett property and seeded in dry-land wheat.

Standing next to the gate, he stared at the old house, recalling someone had told him there'd been a murder there and the house had been boarded up ever since. People liked to make houses seem much more sinister than they actually were, he thought. He was surprised he hadn't heard rumors of ghosts.

But even if nothing evil lurked in that house, it made him wonder what the woman had found so interesting about the place since, from her surprised expression, she hadn't known about the murder.

Hell, maybe she'd never seen an old farmhouse before.

As if he'd ever understood women, he thought, as he climbed back on his four-wheeler, just glad some disaster hadn't befallen her. If all she'd done was leave the gate open then he figured no harm was done. By now, she would be miles away.

Still he couldn't help but wonder what had brought her to his part of Montana in the first place. She certainly was out of her realm, he thought with a chuckle as he headed back to the ranch.

THE WHITEHORSE SEWING Circle was an institution in the county. Jolene had noticed that when the women who spent several days a week at the center making quilts were mentioned, it was with reverence. And maybe a little fear.

Clearly these women had the power in this community. Jolene got the impression that a lot of decisions were made between stitches and a lot of information dispersed over the crisp new fabric of the quilts.

It was with apprehension that she walked over to the center and pushed open the door. She'd been inside before for several get-togethers since she'd been hired as the community's teacher. This was where all the wedding receptions, birthday and anniversary parties, festivals and funeral potlucks were held.

The wooden floors were worn from years of boots dancing across them. It was easy to imagine that hearts had been won and lost in this large open room. A lot of events in these people's lives had been marked here from births to deaths and everything in between. If only these walls could talk, Jolene thought, wondering what stories *they* would tell.

As the door opened, sunlight pouring across the floor, the women all looked in her direction. They were gathered toward the back around a small quilting frame. A baby quilt, she realized, as she let the door close behind her.

"Hello," Pearl Cavanaugh said, smiling her slightly lopsided smile. Pearl had had a stroke sometime back and was still recovering, Jolene had heard. Pearl's mother had started the Whitehorse Sewing Circle years ago, according to the locals.

"I just thought I'd stop in and see what you were making," Jolene said lamely. How was she ever going to get to her true mission in coming here?

She knew she had to be careful. For fear the story might stop, she didn't want the author of the story to find out she'd been asking around about the murder.

"Please. Join us," Pearl said.

The women looked formidable, eyes keen, but their expressions were friendly enough as she pulled up a chair at the edge of the circle and watched their weathered, arthritic hands make the tiniest, most perfect stitches she'd ever seen.

"The quilt is beautiful," she said into the silence. She could feel some of the women studying her discreetly.

"Thank you," Pearl said, clearly the spokeswoman for the group. Her husband, Titus, served as a sort of mayor for Old Town Whitehorse, preaching in the center on Sundays, making sure the cemetery was maintained and overseeing the hiring of teachers as needed.

"You have all met our new teacher, Jolene Stevens,"

Pearl was saying. "She comes to us straight from Montana State University."

"So this is your first teaching assignment," a small white-haired, blue-eyed woman said with a nice smile. "I'm Alice White."

"I recall your birthday party," Jolene said. "Ninety-two, I believe?"

Alice chuckled. "Everyone must think I'm going to kick the bucket sometime soon since they're determined to celebrate my birthday every year now." She winked at Jolene. "What they don't know is that I'm going to live to be a hundred."

Jolene tried to relax in the smattering of laughter that followed. "This area is so interesting. I'm really enjoying the history."

"I'm sure everyone's told you about the famous outlaws who used to hide out in this part of the state at the end of the eighteenth century," a large woman with a cherubic face said. Ella Cavanaugh, a shirttail relation to Pearl and Titus, as Jolene recalled. Everyone seemed to be related in some way or another.

"Butch Cassidy and the Sundance Kid as well as Kid Curry," added another elderly member, Mabel Brown. "This part of the state was lawless back then."

"It certainly seems peaceful enough now," Jolene commented. "But I did hear something about a murder of a young widow who had a little girl, I believe?"

She could have heard a pin drop. Several jaws definitely dropped, but quickly snapped shut again.

"Nasty business that was," Ella said and glanced at Pearl.

"When was it?" Jolene asked, sensing that Pearl was about to shut down the topic.

"Twenty-four years ago this month," Alice said,

shaking her head. "It isn't something any of us likes to think about."

"Was her killer ever caught?" Jolene asked and saw the answer on their faces.

"Do you sew, Jolene?" Pearl asked. "We definitely could use some young eyes and nimble fingers."

"I'm afraid not."

"We would be happy to teach you," Pearl said. "We make quilts for every baby born around here and have for years. It's a Whitehorse tradition."

"A very nice one," Jolene agreed. She had wanted to ask more about the murder, but saw that the rest of the women were now intent on their quilting. Pearl had successfully ended the discussion. "Well, I should leave you to your work," Jolene said, rising to her feet to leave.

"Well, if you ever change your mind," Pearl said, looking up at her questioningly. No doubt she wondered where Jolene had heard about a twenty-four-year-old unsolved murder—and why she would be interested.

As Jolene left, she glanced back at the women. Only one was watching her. Pearl Cavanaugh. She looked troubled.

DULCIE DROVE BACK INTO town, even more curious about her inheritance. She returned to the real-estate office only to find that April was officiating a game at the old high-school gym.

The old gym was built of brick and was cavernous inside. Fortunately, the game hadn't started yet. She found April in uniform on the sidelines.

"I'm sorry to bother you again," Dulcie apologized. "Who would I talk to about the history of the property?"

April thought for a moment. "Talk to Roselee at the

museum. She's old as dirt, but sharp as a tack. She's our local historian."

The small museum was on the edge of town and filled with the history of this part of Montana. Roselee turned out to be a white-haired woman of indeterminable age. She smiled as Dulcie came through the door, greeting her warmly and telling her about the museum.

"Actually, I was interested in the history of a place south of here," Dulcie said. "I heard you might be able to help me."

Roselee looked pleased. "Well, I've been around here probably the longest. My father homesteaded in Old Town Whitehorse."

Even better, Dulcie thought.

"Whose place are we talking about?"

"Laura Beaumont's."

All the friendliness left her voice. "If you're one of those reporters doing another story on the murder—"

"I'm not. But I need to know. Was it Laura Beaumont who was murdered?"

Roselee pursed her lips. "If you're not a reporter, then what is your interest in all this?"

"I inherited the property."

The woman's eyes widened. She groped for the chair behind her and sat down heavily.

Dulcie felt goose bumps ripple across her flesh at the look on the woman's face. "What is it?" she demanded, frightened by the way Roselee was staring at her—as if she'd seen a ghost.

The elderly woman shook her head and struggled to her feet. "I'm sorry. I'm not feeling well." She picked up the cane leaning against the counter and started toward the back of the museum, calling to someone named Cara.

"If I come by some other time?" Dulcie said to the woman's retreating back, but Roselee didn't respond.

What in the world, she thought, as a much younger woman hurried to the counter and asked if she could help.

"Have you ever heard of a woman named Laura Beaumont?" Dulcie asked.

Cara, who was close to Dulcie's age, shook her head. "Should I have?"

"I don't know." Dulcie felt shaken from Roselee's reaction. "Do you have a historical society?"

The young woman broke into a smile. "You just met the president, Roselee." She sobered. "Wasn't she able to help you?"

"No. Is there someone else around town I could talk to?" She dropped her voice just in case Roselee was in the back, listening. "Someone older who knows everything that goes on around here, especially Old Town Whitehorse, and doesn't mind talking about it?"

Cara's eyes shone with understanding. She, too, whispered. "There is someone down south who might be able to help you. Her name is Arlene Evans. She's… talkative."

JOLENE GLANCED AT HER watch as she left the Community Center. If she hurried she could make it into Whitehorse before the newspaper office closed.

Now that she knew there had been a murder, she was anxious to go through the *Milk River Examiner* newspapers from twenty-four years ago to find out everything she could about it.

Back in the schoolhouse, she went to her desk and opened the drawer where she'd put the stories. All six were there. She had yet to read the other five, so she stuffed them all into her backpack.

Turning to leave, she was startled to find a dark shape filling the schoolhouse doorway.

"Sorry, didn't mean to startle you," Ben Carpenter said as he stepped inside. He was a big man who took up a lot of space and always made Jolene feel a little uncomfortable. She suspected it was because he seldom smiled. Ben was at the far end of his forties and the father of her moody eighth-grader, Mace.

"I was just finishing up for the day. Is there something Mace needed?" The boy resembled his father, large and beefy. Jolene had only once seen his mother, Ronda, but recalled she was tiny and reserved.

"I stopped in to see how Mace is doing," Ben said. "I ask him, but he doesn't say much. You aren't having any trouble with him, are you? If you are, you just let me know and I'll see to the boy."

Jolene didn't like the threat she heard in Ben's tone. "He's doing quite well and, no, I have no trouble at all with him."

"Good," Ben said, looking uncomfortable in the small setting. "Glad to hear it. His mother has been after me to find out."

Jolene doubted that. Ronda Carpenter seemed like a woman who asked little of her husband and got even less. "Well, you can certainly reassure her. Mace is doing fine."

Ben nodded, looking as if there was more he wanted to say, but he changed his mind as he stepped toward the door. "Okay, then."

Jolene was relieved when she heard his truck pull away from the front of the school. She felt a little shaken by his visit. Ben always seemed right on the edge of losing his temper. His visit had felt contrived. Was there something else he'd come by for and changed his mind about?

Was it possible he was the author of the murder story? It didn't seem likely, but then some people wrote better than they spoke.

Locking up behind her, she biked to her little house. Then, with the installments of the murder story in her backpack, she got in her car and headed toward Whitehorse.

She took the dirt road out of town. Old Town Whitehorse had been the first settlement called Whitehorse. It had been nearer the Missouri River and the Breaks. That was back when supplies came by riverboat.

Once the railroad came through, five miles to the north, the town migrated to the tracks, taking the name Whitehorse with it.

As Jolene drove, she mentally replayed the conversation with the women of the sewing circle and was even more curious why they had been so reticent to talk about the murder.

RUSSELL FOUND HIS FATHER waiting for him when he returned to the ranch. Grayson Corbett was a large man with graying hair and an easygoing smile as well as attitude. Grayson had raised his five sons single-handedly from the time Russell was small and had done a damned good job.

Actually there was little his father couldn't do. That's why seeing him like this was so hard on Russell.

Worry lines etched Grayson's still-handsome face and seemed to make his blue eyes even paler. Russell knew what he wanted to talk about the moment he saw his father and felt his stomach turn at the thought.

"We have to make a decision," Grayson said without preamble. "We can't put it off any longer." Clearly his father had been thinking about the problem and probably little else since they'd last talked.

"You already know how I feel," Russell said. "It's a damned-fool thing and a waste of money as far as I'm concerned. What did the other ranchers and farmers have to say at the meeting?"

"Some agree with you. But there are more who are ready to try anything if there's a chance of saving their crops."

Russell shook his head, seeing that his father had already made his decision.

"If some of these farmers and ranchers don't get some moisture and soon, they're going to lose everything," Grayson said. "I don't think we have a choice."

"So what did you tell them?"

"I told them I had to talk to my son," his father said. "This is your ranch as much as mine, more actually. You get the final word."

Russell could see that his father was worried about the others, who had the most to lose. "What choice do we have?"

If he and his father didn't go along with the rest, he doubted the fifteen thousand dollars needed to hire the rainmaker could be raised. "I'll go along with whatever decision you make."

Grayson looked relieved, not that the worry lines softened. They were throwing good money away, Russell believed. But if the ranchers and farmers wanted to believe some man could make rain, then he wasn't going to try to stop them.

"Thank you," Grayson said as he laid a heavy hand

on his son's shoulders. "At least by hiring a rainmaker, they feel they're doing something to avert disaster."

THE *MILK RIVER EXAMINER* was the only newspaper for miles around. It was housed in a small building along the main street facing the tracks.

Andi Blake, the paper's only reporter, a friendly, attractive woman with a southern accent, helped Jolene.

"What date are you looking for?" Andi asked.

Jolene told her it would have been this month twenty-four years ago. "I'm not sure of the exact date."

"I wasn't here then, but you're welcome to look. Everything is on microfiche. You know how to use it?"

Jolene did from her college days. She thanked Andi, then sat down in the back of the office and, as the articles from May twenty-four years ago began to come up on screen, she began to roll her way through.

She slowed at the stories about the drought conditions, the fears of the ranchers and farmers, talk of hiring a rainmaker to come to town. A few papers later, there was a small article about a rainmaker coming to town and how the ranchers were raising money to pay him to make rain.

With a shudder, Jolene thought of the murder story and her feeling that the weather conditions were too much like this year.

The headline in the very next newspaper stopped her cold.

Woman Murdered in Brutal Attack

An Old Town Whitehorse resident was found murdered in her home last evening.

Heart in her throat, Jolene read further, then backtracked, realizing that the article didn't say who found the body.

The sheriff was asking anyone with information in connection to the murder of Laura Beaumont to come forward.

If this Laura Beaumont was the same woman that the author of the murder story was writing about, she had at least one lover.

Their DNA would have been in the house. But had law enforcement even heard of DNA testing twenty-four years ago? It wouldn't have been widely used even if they had. Certainly not in Whitehorse.

Jolene continued to read, halting on the next paragraph.

The woman was found upstairs in her bed. She had been stabbed numerous times.

Had her lover found her? Or—

Sheriff's deputies are searching for the woman's missing young daughter.

Missing?

Angel Beaumont is about four or five years old with brown hair and eyes. It is unknown what she might have been wearing at the time of her disappearance.

Jolene quickly flipped to the next weekly newspaper and scanned for an article about the murder. The girl was *still* missing a week later?

Searchers are combing the creek behind the farmhouse for the girl's body, but with no sign of the daughter. If anyone knows of the child's whereabouts or has information about the killing, they are to contact the sheriff's department at once. All calls will be confidential.

A few issues later, Jolene found the news article about the daughter.

DULCIE GRABBED SOMETHING to eat at a small café downtown and debated if she should call this Arlene Evans woman or drive out to her place. She opted to drive out unannounced and talk to her face-to-face.

As she was leaving the café, her mind on what she would say once she reached the Evans place, Dulcie bumped into a young woman coming out of one of the local businesses.

"Pardon me," Dulcie said as the woman, slim, dark-haired and pretty, dropped the folder she'd been carrying. Papers fluttered across the sidewalk. "I'm so sorry."

Dulcie hurried to help her pick up the scattered sheets, noticing that they were copies of newspaper articles. One headline caught her eye. *Investigation Continues in Murder Case.*

"Thank you," the young woman said, clearly upset as she hurriedly stuffed the copies back into the folder and rushed to her compact car parked at the curb.

Murder? Dulcie wondered how many murders they had in a town like this and what were the chances the article could have been about Laura Beaumont. She told herself that when she had more time and information, she'd come back and have a look at some old newspaper stories.

As she climbed into her rental car, she put the incident out of her mind and drove south to the Evans place outside of Old Town Whitehorse.

Like everything else in this part of Montana, the houses were few and far between, with a lot of prairie and gullies and sagebrush to fill the spaces.

It was late and Dulcie wasn't sure what approach to use when she knocked on the farmhouse door.

"Arlene Evans?" she asked the tall, rawboned ranchwoman who answered the door. Her hair was short in a becoming style that made her appear younger than Dulcie had expected.

"Yes?"

"I'm looking for some information and I was hoping you could help me."

"I'll certainly try. Why don't you step in out of the heat? I just made some lemonade. Would you like a glass?"

Dulcie blinked in surprise at how easy it had been to get inside this woman's home. Had this been Chicago and a stranger knocking on Dulcie's door…well, she wouldn't have opened it, let alone invited her inside for lemonade.

Dulcie noticed photographs on the wall of what appeared to be Arlene's grown children. The oldest looked to be in her thirties and rather frumpy. A woman in her early twenties was posing with a baby in her arms and a young man, presumably her husband, standing next to her. They looked as if they were crazy about each other. The third photo was of a handsome young man, but there was something sneaky in his gaze.

"Is this about my rural online dating service?" Arlene asked from the kitchen. "Have a seat," she said, motioning to the adjacent living room as she came in, and handed Dulcie a tall glass of lemonade.

It looked so good she took a sip before she sat down in the immaculate house. "This is wonderful," she said, licking her lips.

Arlene Evans smiled as she sat down across from her. The house was surprisingly cool, considering how hot it was outside.

"An online rural dating service? That does sound interesting, but I'm here about something else," Dulcie said. "Let me be candid with you. I am up here looking at a piece of property." It was the truth. Just not as much truth as she'd told Roselee at the museum. She didn't want another reaction like that one.

"Property?" Arlene repeated.

"I'm trying to find out the history of the place. I understand you've lived here all your life and might be able to help me."

"Well, like I said, I'll certainly try."

Dulcie noticed the ring on Arlene's finger as she put down her lemonade glass on one of the coasters on the coffee table. "That's a beautiful ring."

"Thank you. I'm getting married in a few months. A Christmas wedding."

"Congratulations." The diamond was extraordinary, and Dulcie wondered if Arlene was marrying some rich rancher from around here.

"So where is this property?"

"It's outside Old Town Whitehorse. I believe the last occupant of the place was named Laura Beaumont?"

"Oh, my gosh." Arlene's expression told her that she'd hit paydirt.

"Did you know Laura?"

"Not personally. I knew she was widowed. She wasn't from around here and wasn't here all that long. I heard the land belonged to her husband's family and was all that she had, so she had no choice but to live here after her husband died. She leased all of the farmland. Clearly she had no interest in farming or living in the country."

Arlene seemed to catch herself. "I shouldn't be saying anything because I didn't know her. You know how rumors get started."

Apparently Arlene was trying to live down her reputation as a gossip. "Do you know where Laura moved from?" asked Dulcie.

"California. That was another reason it was odd. Californians move to Montana all the time, just not this part of Montana, if you know what I mean."

She did. California though? Not the Chicago area. So how was it that her parents knew this woman?

"Can you tell me what happened to her?"

"You don't *know?*"

Dulcie wanted to hear it from Arlene. "Please, I really need you to be honest with me. I heard she might have been murdered?"

"Well, it's not like I'm carrying tales. Everyone knows. She was murdered in one of the upstairs bedrooms twenty…oh, my gosh, twenty-four years ago this month!"

Did that explain why Roselee at the museum had gotten so upset? "Murder must be rare in this part of the country," she said, thinking of the woman she'd run into earlier with the copies of the newspaper clippings about a murder.

"It *is* rare, but this murder…" Arlene shook her head. "It was quite vicious. She was stabbed to death over a dozen times and the killer was never caught."

Dulcie was trying to take this all in when Arlene said, "What made it all the more horrific was her daughter."

"Her *daughter?*"

"She was just a little thing, four or five, as I recall. They discovered her bloody footprints in the bedroom where she'd come in. She must have seen her mother lying there and ran."

Chapter Four

Kate Corbett saw at once that her oldest stepson wasn't himself at supper. The quietest of the five brothers, Russell also was the most grounded. He was the one who'd gone into ranching with his father right out of college. Grayson couldn't manage without Russell working the ranches with him so Kate was thankful for that.

When Grayson had sold out his holdings in Texas and moved to Montana, his sons had been shocked and blamed Kate, she knew.

Later when Grayson had asked them all to come to Montana for a family meeting, the other four had come, but not happily.

Fortunately that had changed, she thought, as she glanced around the supper table at the large family she'd married into. It had grown since they'd all been in Montana.

The second oldest, Lantry Corbett, was a divorce lawyer of all things. And while he was still in Montana on the ranch, Kate didn't expect him to stay.

Shane Corbett, the next oldest, had been on medical leave from the Texas Rangers. Kate knew that if he hadn't fallen in love with a local girl, he would have returned to Texas.

Instead, he'd hired on with the Whitehorse sheriff's

department as a deputy. He and Maddie Cavanaugh had recently married in a triple wedding with his twin brothers, Jud and Dalton.

Kate certainly hadn't seen that coming, but she couldn't have been happier to see the daughter she'd never known so happy. She and Maddie had some things to work out still, but they had time, Kate told herself.

Jud was the youngest, but only by a few minutes of his fraternal twin, Dalton. Jud had been working as a stuntman in Hollywood but had fallen in love with Faith Bailey while shooting a film in Montana. The two had started a stunt-riding school on her family ranch not far from Trails West Ranch.

Dalton had fallen for the owner of the local knit shop, Georgia Michaels. That one Kate *had* seen coming and she and Grayson couldn't be more pleased.

Even though the three sons had married, they and their wives were living on the ranch until their houses could be completed. It was wonderful having such a full table and Juanita, the cook Grayson had talked into making the move to Montana, loved it. She'd outdone herself each meal, wanting to make the new brides feel at home here.

Marriage, surprisingly, was what had brought Grayson's sons to Montana. For years after his wife, Rebecca, had died, leaving him with five young sons to raise, Grayson hadn't been able to go through Rebecca's things. Nor did anyone expect him to remarry.

Kate and Rebecca had been best friends, growing up together on the Trails West Ranch in Montana until Kate's father grew ill and died, the ranch lost.

Kate also lost track of her friend who'd married Grayson Corbett and moved to Texas. It wasn't until Kate found some old photographs of Rebecca that she decided to pay Grayson a visit.

There had been a spark between them from the moment they'd met. In a whirlwind romance, they'd married and Grayson had surprised her by buying Trails West Ranch for her and moving lock, stock and barrel to Montana as a wedding present.

That was when Grayson finally went through Rebecca's things and found some old letters she had written before she died.

In a letter to Grayson, Rebecca had explained that she'd written five letters, one for each son, to be read on his wedding day. Her dying wish was that her sons would marry before thirty-five—and that the bride be a Montana cowgirl.

While Kate had heard that the brothers drew straws to see who would fulfill their mother's wishes first, she'd known the brothers well enough to know they would try to get out of the pact. But amazingly, she'd seen Rebecca's wishes coming true with all but two of her sons.

Although Lantry had no intention of ever marrying, he hadn't left the ranch. What had made them stay, Kate felt, was family.

As for Russell, well, she believed he'd never met a woman who interested him enough to want to pursue her.

Kate and Grayson had had a few rough spots since their marriage, but everything had finally settled down.

That's why seeing this change in Russell intrigued her.

"How was your day?" she asked Russell now, curious.

He'd been smiling to himself all through the meal. Normally he ate quickly and went back to work, excusing himself by saying he had too much to do to just sit around.

Tonight, though, he seemed lost in thought, unusually distracted, especially since his father and the rest of the ranchers and farmers were worried sick about the lack of moisture this spring.

"Fine." He looked bashful suddenly. Like his father and brothers he was a very good-looking man, with Grayson's dark hair and his mother's intense blue eyes.

"Nothing *unusual* happened?" Kate probed.

Russell realized that everyone was staring at him, waiting.

"Nothing *happened*. I just almost killed some city girl today."

"What?" Kate exclaimed.

"Don't worry, she was unscathed." At everyone's urging, he told them about coming over a rise in the combine, not expecting anyone to be on the road since no one had lived in the old Beaumont place for years and the road dead-ended a mile up.

"She was sitting in her fancy rental car, right in the middle of the road on her *cell phone*," he said, getting the appropriate chuckles and head shakes. Kate could tell he was embarrassed, not used to being the center of attention in this family.

"Where was she from?" Grayson asked.

"Midwest, from her accent, but definitely big city. You should have seen the shoes she was wearing." Russell shook his head. "And when she tried to open the gate…"

"Open the gate to where?" Shane wanted to know.

"The old Beaumont place, isn't that what it's called?"

"Why would she go in there?" his father wanted to know.

"Beats me. It's what she wanted so I opened the gate for her. I warned her it was private property. She didn't seem to care. I think she thought I was joking when I told her about the rattlesnakes."

"Oh, I hope she was all right," Kate said, worried. "You just left her there?"

Russell laughed, seeming to relax, maybe even enjoy himself. "She wasn't like a stray dog I was going to bring home."

"Still, if she was that inept, she could get herself into trouble."

Russell nodded. "I'm sure she will, but believe me, she didn't want my help—or my advice."

No, Kate thought, she was sure the woman hadn't, but city girl or not, she'd certainly made an impression on Russell—something not easy to do.

DULCIE SHUDDERED. Laura Beaumont's young daughter had found her body? That poor child. That poor, poor child.

The horrible dread Dulcie had felt earlier at the farmhouse swept over again.

I wasn't that little girl.

Where had that come from? Of course she wasn't Laura Beaumont's daughter. Why had she even thought such a thing?

Just because of her earlier reaction to yellow curtains and the groaning weather vane? Just because she couldn't shake the sense of dread and fear?

Or because of the obvious? She'd *inherited* the property from a woman she'd never heard of and a woman her parents had never mentioned to her.

Dulcie recalled Renada's reaction when she'd told her. She cleared her throat. "How old did you say this child was?"

"Four or five, I think. I'm not sure anyone knew for sure."

Four or five would make the child about twenty-eight or twenty-nine now. Dulcie had just turned twenty-eight.

"What was the daughter's name?"

"Angel."

Angel. Dulcie felt a surge of relief that lasted only an instant. Of course the girl's name would have been changed if she was adopted.

Dulcie couldn't believe what she was thinking, but the kids at school and even their parents used to ask her if she was adopted because her parents were so much older than the other parents.

But if she'd been adopted, her parents would have told her. They wouldn't have kept something like that from her.

Like the way they kept the property in Montana from her?

Her heart began to pound as she thought of her elderly parents, her mother's years of trying to conceive without any luck, her mother finally getting Dulcie so late in life. Miracle? Or lie?

Everything could be a lie, including her real name.

"What happened to the daughter?" Dulcie had to ask.

Arlene sighed. "She was found drowned a couple weeks after her mother's murder."

The shock reverberated through her.

"They found her under some brush in the creek. She's

buried at the cemetery at Old Town Whitehorse next to her mother."

Dulcie was so stunned it took her a moment to speak. "She's *dead?*" She couldn't be Angel Beaumont. She thought of the little girl and felt horrible for the moment of relief she'd experienced.

Arlene nodded solemnly. "It was a horrible tragedy, both mother and daughter."

"Do they think the killer—"

"No," Arlene said quickly. "The sheriff said she had fallen and hit her head and drowned. The creek wasn't very deep that spring. It had been very hot and dry."

Dulcie felt shaken. The mother murdered, the daughter killed in a freak accident. It still didn't explain how Dulcie had inherited the property. Or why she'd reacted the way she had when she'd seen the yellow curtains in that second-floor window and heard the tortured sound of the weather vane.

She downed the cold drink in her hand, suddenly exhausted. "Thank you for the lemonade. It was delicious."

"So will you buy the property?" Arlene asked as Dulcie rose to leave.

She could see that the woman was curious about Dulcie's real reason for asking about Laura Beaumont and her daughter. Maybe even more curious why she'd want the property.

"I hope I haven't dissuaded you."

"Not at all," Dulcie said. "I'm going to sleep on it. I couldn't make any kind of a decision as tired as I am."

She left Arlene and drove back to Whitehorse. It had gotten dark, the sky deepening from dove gray to an inky black devoid of moon or stars, as if the heat had melted them. She tried not to think as she let the car's air-conditioning blow on her, but her mind raced anyway.

She *wasn't* Angel Beaumont. But it gave her no peace. Laura murdered, her daughter, Angel, drowned in the creek, the property left to Dulcie—a little girl herself at the time. Something was wrong with all this, she could feel it.

As she passed through town, the temperature sign on the bank read eighty-four degrees. It was going to be another miserably hot night.

She chose the first motel she came to on the edge of town. Once inside her room, she showered, turned up the air conditioner and lay down on the bed.

She thought about calling Renada, but didn't feel up to it even though there was a message from her friend. Tomorrow, when she didn't feel so exhausted, so depressed. If she called her now, Renada would hear how discouraged she was and insist on coming out to Montana. Anyway, it was too late to call with the time difference between here and Chicago.

Dulcie expected to fall into a deep sleep almost instantly, as tired as she was. But when she closed her eyes, she saw the yellow curtains move in the upstairs bedroom and heard the groan of the weather vane on the barn in the hot, dry wind.

All she could think about was that little girl. That poor little girl.

JOLENE WOKE TO DARKNESS and sat up, startled, to find she'd fallen asleep in her living-room chair.

The pages from the short stories fluttered to the floor at her feet as she reached for the lamp next to her chair and checked the time.

Well after midnight. She must have been more tired

than she'd thought. She blamed the relentless heat, which had zapped her energy and left her feeling like a wrung-out dishrag.

Even this late, the air in the small house was hot and close. She felt clammy and yearned for a breath of cool air as she turned up the fan in the window. All it did was blow in warm air, but even warm air was better than nothing.

As she leaned down to retrieve the stories, she caught sight of the murder story.

Her fingers slowed as she reached for it, remembering with a start what she'd learned at the newspaper. Widow Laura Beaumont had been murdered twenty-four years ago and she, like the woman in the supposedly fictional murder story, had a young daughter.

A daughter who'd been found drowned in the creek.

The short story had to be about the same woman and her child, didn't it?

She put the critiqued story installments into her backpack, although she wouldn't be returning them until the entire story had been finished, turned in and graded.

She didn't want to stifle their creativity with her comments on the earlier assignments, although her comments were very complimentary of their endeavors. The idea was to encourage her students to write freely. She understood the fear some people had about putting words to paper.

As she zipped up the backpack, she looked down at the murder story on the table where she'd left it. She would hide it in the house for now. She didn't want to take the chance that someone would find it in the schoolhouse and read it.

The story was becoming more and more like *her* dark

secret and that should have made her even more uneasy than it did, she thought.

As she headed to bed, Jolene realized that the author of the murder story had gotten to her. Not only couldn't she wait for the next part, but she now felt personally involved in solving the mystery.

Reading Monday's and Tuesday's assignments in order, she had looked for some clue as to the writer. Was the writer just someone with an active imagination? Or a local gossip who thought she knew what had happened that summer, if indeed the story was about Laura Beaumont and her daughter, Angel?

There was nothing in the story that would make Jolene believe it had been written by the killer, she assured herself.

So why did the details in the story make her so nervous? Because if she was right, the author had known this woman. Had watched the murdered woman closely. Just as the writer might be watching right now to see Jolene's reaction, she realized with a chill as she snapped off the light.

DULCIE WOKE WEDNESDAY morning after sleeping later than she had in years. It surprised her given how much trouble she'd had getting to sleep last night.

She'd told Arlene Evans the truth. She'd had to sleep on it before making a decision as to what to do about the property.

Common sense told her to just list the property with the Realtor she'd met and return to Chicago and start seriously looking for her next business venture.

But even as she thought it, Dulcie knew she couldn't leave without going into that house. She had to know if she'd been there before.

She groaned at the thought. She would need to buy appropriate clothing for exploring, along with gloves, a flashlight and tools to get into the house. She sat down and made a list before heading to the local clothing and hardware stores.

"You say you'll be removing boards?" Kayla at the hardware store inquired. "You'll want a hammer and pry bar for sure, but possibly a crowbar or even a battery-operated screwdriver. Are these large boards, nailed or screwed?"

By the time Dulcie left the hardware store, she felt equipped for an exploration to Antarctica. Kayla had suggested canvas pants and a jacket as well as work boots, and Dulcie thanked her for all her help.

Back at the motel, she changed and, putting all her equipment in the trunk, drove south. The moment the farmhouse came into view, she felt that now-familiar sense of dread and fear wash over her.

She almost changed her mind and turned around. She was even more persuaded against staying when she saw that someone had closed the damned gate.

JOLENE WATCHED AS Thad Brooks, one of her fifth-grade boys, collected the writing assignments. She'd felt antsy all morning, waiting for the next installment of the murder story, afraid this would be the day that the story stopped as mysteriously as it had begun.

She could hear the dried grasses outside the open window rustling in the hot, dry wind and fanned herself as the student placed the stack of papers on the edge of her desk.

"How are you all doing on your stories?" she asked and listened to a variety of complaints from being stuck to being bored.

"At this point in your stories, I want you to sit down and write down ten things that could happen next," she told the class. "When you get stuck and can't think of anything else to write about your character, it helps if you do what is called brainstorming. Let your imagination run as you write down as many things as you can think of that could happen."

"What if you can't think of anything?" whined Luke Raines, her other fifth-grader.

"Then you have to think harder. Concentrate. Think about your characters. Think about the weather. Think about where you are in the story. The middle parts are the hardest because you have to keep the story going. It helps if something exciting happens that changes the direction of your story. What is the worst thing that could happen to your characters? What is your hero or heroine most afraid of? For instance, what if there was a huge storm? What if your character was caught in it? What if someone new came to town? What if some old enemy came to town? What if your character found out a secret?"

Jolene saw Mace Carpenter writing like crazy. Amy Brooks was also writing. Thad and Luke were mugging faces at each other. Codi Fox was staring at the ceiling, but Jolene could see her mind working.

"I need the next segment of your stories tomorrow, so keep up the momentum."

"Do we really have to write something every night this week?" Thad asked.

"Yes—and this weekend you will write the ending, to be turned in on Monday for a total of six parts of the story."

Thad and Luke groaned.

"That's why you have to brainstorm more ideas,"

Jolene said. "Open your mind to new possibilities. What kind of trouble can your character get into? Today is only Wednesday. You have another night. Now make a list. I want at least ten things that could happen before you leave today."

She waited until each student had at least ten things written down before she dismissed the students for recess. She hadn't planned to read any of the stories until later at home. But she had to see if the murder story was in the stack.

Hurriedly she thumbed through them, trying to keep an eye on the door just in case one of the parents should stop by. Ben Carpenter's visit yesterday had spooked her. That and realizing that the author of the story was probably *now* keeping an eye on her just as he had Laura Beaumont, twenty-four years ago.

She was trying to imagine Ben authoring the story when, with a start, she realized the murder-story installment wasn't in the stack.

Frantically, she leafed through the stack again, this time more slowly. With relief she found it sandwiched between sixth-grader Codi Fox's and eighth-grader Mace Carpenter's.

Her heart sped up again. Had Mace turned this in with his? Then she remembered that Luke Raines had been gathering the assignments and putting some on the top of the stack and others on the bottom.

She thought about picking up the assignments herself tomorrow, but that might alert whichever student was bringing the extra copy. No, she didn't want to call attention by changing things. The chosen student enjoyed being the one who got to collect the papers each day. Tomorrow though, she would pay more attention when the student was collecting the stories.

She pulled out the murder story, glancing toward the door before she read the installment quickly, guiltily.

Dusk had settled over the land, but the heat was relentless as her lover sneaked away from the old farmhouse, believing she loved him and only him.

She stood at the window and watched him go, but he hadn't gone far down the road before a restlessness overtook her again.

She pulled the lightweight yellow robe around her. Her favorite color, yellow. She liked it because she said it made her feel good.

Colors altered her moods, she said. Green calmed her. Blue made her nostalgic. Red, well, red made her amorous. As if she needed any encouragement.

He hadn't been gone long, the air stifling, heat radiating up from the baked, dry earth, before she poured herself a bath.

She slipped down into the big claw-footed tub full of cool water and closed her eyes. Her fingers teased the water around her body as she daydreamed of another life far away from this dusty, hot farmhouse.

In the next room, her daughter played quietly, ignoring the sound of the vehicle that pulled into the yard, the heavy footfalls on the stairs, the creak of the bathroom door as it opened and closed.

As voices rose from an argument behind the bathroom door, the little girl covered her ears and sang a song her mommy had taught her until she heard the bathroom door slam open and the angry footfalls on the stairs again, and finally the sound of her mother crying softly across the hall.

RUSSELL CORBETT COULDN'T believe his eyes. The city girl's rental car was parked in front of the old Beaumont place again.

But that wasn't what had him throwing on the brakes and skidding to a dust-boiling stop.

The woman had a crowbar in her gloved hands and appeared to be trying to remove the boards barring the front door.

"What the hell do you think you're doing?" he demanded as he strode past the gate lying oddly in the dead grass. "Tell me you didn't cut the barbed wire on that gate to get in here."

She turned slowly to give him a droll look. "Okay."

He snatched his gray Stetson from his head and smacked it against his jean-clad thigh in irritation. "You can't go around cutting people's gates and vandalizing their property, even if it is abandoned."

She cocked her head as if seeing him for the first time. He was starting to lose his temper when she said calmly, "This *is* my property."

"What?" He thought he had to have heard her wrong.

Smiling, she nodded, seeming to enjoy his surprise and loss of words.

"You *bought* this place?" he asked, his tone making it clear nothing could make him believe she wanted to live here.

Her hands went to her hips, the crowbar hooked between the fingers of her right hand. "I'm sorry, I missed the part where it was your business."

The woman had some mouth on her, he thought, his gaze going to her bow-shaped, full pink lips. His own lips twitched in response to the mad detour his mind took as it tried to imagine what it would be like to kiss that mouth of hers.

He held up his hands in surrender. "Don't let me keep you then." He started to turn away, planning to stalk back to his four-wheeler, cursing all the way under his breath.

"Wait. I'm sorry. I'm just hot and frustrated." She sighed. "I can't seem to get this last board to come loose. Since you're here, would you mind?"

He pulled up short, her soft, seductive tone like a lasso dragging him back. He told himself to keep walking. If he turned around he'd regret it. This woman was trouble in a pair of dirt-smudged canvas pants.

Turning slowly, he eyed her from under the brim of his hat the way he would eye a rattler about to strike. He didn't trust this change of tune on her part. She couldn't get the last board so now she was going to turn on the feminine charms, thinking they would work on him?

"I wouldn't want to make it my *business*."

She transformed that magnificent mouth of hers into a lazy grin. One hand was on her shapely hips now, the other beckoning him with the crowbar. "I *said* I was sorry."

He felt himself weaken in spite of every instinct to keep his distance from this one. But he'd been born and raised in Texas, where a man came to the aid of a lady. Although it was debatable this woman was a lady.

"I really would appreciate it," she said in that same come-hither tone. "This last board just won't budge."

Russell let out a deep sigh, mentally kicking himself in the behind, as he stepped to her, took the crowbar from her without a word and pried off the board, the nails screeching as they gave way.

He tossed the board to the side where she'd thrown the others and handed her back the crowbar. The plan was to tip his hat like the gentleman he was and get the hell out of there without looking back.

"Dulcie Hughes," she said, tugging off her glove and holding out one perfectly manicured hand.

He slowly wiped his hand on his jeans and extended it grudgingly, telling himself he wasn't going to let her rope him into anything else. For all he knew the woman could be lying about owning this place and he'd just helped her commit a crime.

Her hand was cool and smooth as porcelain as it disappeared into his larger, calloused one. "Russell Corbett," he said, his voice sounding as rough as his hand.

Her molasses-brown-eyed gaze met his. Humor seemed to jitterbug in all that warm brown. "Thank you, Russell Corbett. I do apologize for earlier. I hate it when I can't handle something myself. It makes me testy."

He nodded, familiar with that feeling.

"So what is a Southern boy like yourself doing out here in Montana?" she said, smiling.

He told himself he had work to do and no time for standing around in this heat chitchatting, but he'd pay hell before being rude to a woman.

"I came up from Texas to work the Trails West Ranch." He made a motion with his head to the west, wondering why he hadn't told her he was co-owner of the family ranch. Because it was none of her *business*.

"I take it the ranch is down the road apiece?" she asked with a grin. "Everything up here seems to be down the road apiece."

He couldn't tell if she was having fun at his expense or not. Whatever she was doing, she seemed to be enjoying herself and he kind of liked her when she wasn't on her high horse.

She wiped a hand across her forehead, skin glistening in the heat, and left a smudge of dirt just above one finely sculpted eyebrow. It made her look a little less in control, something he thought probably rare.

"Mind if I ask what you're planning to do here?" He gestured toward the house.

"Just going to take a look around, then put the place up for sale. I inherited it sight unseen and was just curious."

"Inherited it, huh. Is your family from around here?"

"No. Would you be interested in buying the property?"

He noticed the way she had quickly changed the subject. "Might be interested. So you aren't related to the Beaumonts?"

"Did you know the woman who lived here? The one who was murdered?"

"Before my time." Russell was getting tired of her not answering his questions, but then again, who was he to ask? He started to leave, but couldn't help himself. "If you're determined to go in there, you should know the floors might be rotted through, rattlers probably have nested inside, not to mention bats and mice and every other rodent known to man."

She cocked her head at him. "You like scaring me, don't you?"

"Just trying to give you some friendly advice, which is clear you aren't going to heed." He took a step back, telling himself that no matter what she said or did, he was out of there. She wasn't his responsibility.

"THANKS FOR THE ADVICE," Dulcie said to his retreating backside. Not a bad backside. For the first time, she understood the expression "cowboy swagger."

The man *was* blessed. Not only did he have the looks, he came fully equipped with broad, strong shoulders, slim hips and long legs. And damn but didn't he look good in his Western attire.

She couldn't help grinning as she watched him kick a small stone with the toe of his boot, sending it flying into the sizzling heat. Her grin broadened as she listened to him mutter under his breath just as he had last time.

"Stop by anytime," she called after him and smiled as she watched him swing a leg over his four-wheeler, crank up the engine and take off without a backward glance, the tires throwing gravel.

An errant thought idled past. She hoped she got to see Russell Corbett on a horse before she left town. The man was classic cowboy. What the devil was he doing on a four-wheeler? She shook her head, disappointed to have her illusions about the West and real cowboys crushed.

This time tomorrow she would be flying back to Chicago. Russell Corbett would be just a memory, the only pleasant one she feared she would take from Montana.

With growing dread, Dulcie turned back toward the house and the job ahead of her. Russell Corbett was wrong. It wasn't morbid curiosity that drove her. She just hoped he was wrong as well about the rotten floorboards and the critters nesting inside.

Among the documents her parents' lawyer had given her she'd found a key. She'd assumed it was for the front door. Taking it from the pocket of her new canvas pants, she tried it in the lock. The key turned as if the lock had been opened only yesterday—not over twenty-four years ago.

A still, breathless silence had settled in along with the heat. Dulcie listened for a moment to the steady, quickened beat of her heart, then grasping the knob, she slowly turned it and felt the door begin to swing in.

Chapter Five

"What do you know about the old Beaumont place?" Russell asked his father when Grayson met up with him later.

Grayson seemed distracted for a moment as he pulled his gaze away from the cloudless sky. "Not much. Why do you ask?"

"I just met the owner. At least she claims she's the owner. She says she might be putting the place up for sale."

Grayson studied his son. "*She?* This isn't the city girl you were telling us about at supper, is it?"

"One and the same." He shook his head. "She's over there now exploring that old house."

Grayson looked worried. "By herself? Son, do you think that's wise?"

Russell snorted. "I think it's crazier than hell. But the woman doesn't take advice well."

His father laughed. "What woman does? Maybe it's the way you gave it though. If she's serious about selling that property, I definitely think we should make an offer. That land connects up with ours and has laid fallow all these years. I think we could get a pretty good wheat crop out of it, not to mention the property's got water on it. Why don't you see what she wants for the place," Grayson said, rubbing his jaw.

Russell studied his father for a moment in the dim light of the barn. "You talk to the other ranchers and farmers?"

Grayson nodded. "We all kept telling ourselves that we're bound to get some moisture, but every day it seems to be hotter and drier. If we don't get some rain soon…"

Hiring a rainmaker was a desperate measure and they both knew it. Russell remembered so-called rainmakers being run out of town in Texas after they failed to make it rain and talk had turned violent.

"They've suggested a rainmaker who's been here before," Grayson said, reaching into his pocket to pull out a slip of paper. "I got his name and number."

"I'll make the call," Russell said and saw his father's relief as he handed over the information.

One inch of rain was worth a million dollars in this part of the country. Fifteen thousand to make it rain was cheap. If this Finnegan Amherst could make it rain, then he would be worth every penny.

"And go check on that woman," Grayson said as he started to leave. "Make her an offer she can't refuse," he added with a wink.

DULCIE PUSHED THE DOOR of the old house all the way open and was hit with a blast of stale, putrid air. She recoiled, questioning her sanity. Did she really have to go into this house? What more could she hope to learn about the former owner and her daughter in a house that had been empty for the past twenty-four years?

She didn't know, but she had to find out what the connection was between her and Laura Beaumont. If it was in this house, then she had to look. This was *her* house now, she reminded herself.

Screwing up her courage, she took a tentative step inside. Instantly she was as fascinated as she'd been when she'd looked in the window the day before. The house seemed to have been frozen in time. Nothing out of place. Obviously forensics hadn't torn the house apart like they would have nowadays at a crime scene.

She tried the floorboards, testing them with her weight as she recalled what Russell Corbett had said and mugged a face at the thought. The man was infuriating, but he had gotten her into the house, and for that she would forgive him his oh-so-male arrogance.

The dusty, worn wooden floor creaked and groaned a little, but seemed solid enough as Dulcie entered the room. She left the front door open for the air. Even hot air from outside was better than nothing. It also let in light so she could see better. Both good reasons, although the truth was she wanted the door wide-open in case she needed to make a run for it.

The living room was just as it had appeared through the window. She moved slowly through the room, trying to imagine the woman who'd lived here sitting in that chair with the glass and book next to it on the table.

How was it possible that she had been left this property and knew nothing about Laura Beaumont or her daughter? Her parents must have befriended the woman, helped her out maybe through some organization.

As kind and generous as her parents had been, Dulcie was convinced that had to be it. At some point, her parents must have come up here after the murder and brought four-year-old Dulcie with them. That would explain these odd almost-memories she kept feeling.

Laura, wanting to repay the Hugheses, had in turn left

all she had in the world to them. It was a great scenario except for one thing. Laura Beaumont hadn't left her worldly possessions to Dulcie's parents. She'd left this house and land to Dulcie.

That, she reminded herself, was what worried her. No one left property to a four-year-old unless it was their own child.

At the kitchen door, she stopped, shocked by what she saw. Dishes still on the table. A bowl and a spoon in front of one chair, an overturned cereal box and what appeared to be signs of those critters Russell had told her about.

In front of the other chair was a small plate with a knife next to it and a coffee cup. Dulcie could imagine two shadowy figures sitting there, the daughter having cereal, the mother having toast and coffee. Neither having a clue how horribly this day would end.

She blinked and drew back, knowing she was putting off going upstairs. She'd been afraid that the house would feel familiar, that she would remember being inside here.

But as she stood there, she realized she felt nothing. She hadn't been *inside* this house. At least she couldn't recall this part of the house.

Retracing her footsteps, she moved to the bottom of the stairs and looked up. With the shutters closed up there, it was much darker at the top of the stairs.

Dulcie hesitated. She'd been called bold and daring because of her business ventures. But when it came to this sort of thing, she was far from fearless. She had a yellow streak a mile wide.

Unfortunately, she also possessed a stubborn streak that, while it had seen her through some tough times, right now meant she wasn't leaving here until she went upstairs. So she might as well get it over with.

She clutched the banister, then quickly let go, grimacing as she brushed the cobwebs from her hand onto her canvas pants. Testing each stair with a tentative step, she climbed upward into the dim darkness.

A FEW OF THE LOCALS HAD stopped by right after Jolene was hired to finish out the school term for the teacher who'd run off and gotten married. The locals had brought homemade bread, cinnamon rolls and homemade canned goods from their root cellars.

She'd felt welcomed by their visits and their gifts.

But now as she saw Midge Atkinson drive up in front of her house, Jolene wanted to hide and pretend she wasn't home.

Unfortunately, she feared Midge had seen her pedal down the road from the school only moments before.

From the window, Jolene watched Midge climb out of her SUV and glance around as if looking for a charging dog. Or looking to see if anyone was watching her. She carried a wicker basket to Jolene's front door and knocked.

Making sure that the murder story was carefully hidden in a bottom drawer and the house was neat enough for visitors, Jolene answered the door.

"Hello," she greeted her guest warmly. She'd been warned about Midge Atkinson.

Midge's husband, John, owned half the businesses in town and Midge spent the money from them, was the way Jolene had heard it. "No one crosses the Atkinsons," one woman had whispered conspiratorially to her. "Midge likes to wield her power. I don't think I have to tell you who wears the pants in that family."

As a matter of fact, Midge was wearing pants today, a pair of purple ones with a matching large, garish print blouse. "I brought you a little something," she said, slipping past Jolene and into the house without waiting to be asked.

As Jolene closed the door, she noticed Midge inspecting the place. Her visitor's gaze fell on the table where Jolene had left the students' short stories she still had to read.

"Here, let me take that," Jolene said of the basket Midge was holding. She set it down on the table and quickly put the stories into her backpack, zipping it closed. "Please sit down. What can I get you to drink?"

"I can't stay long," Midge said as she took a seat near the fan in the window. "Something cool to drink would be nice though."

"I have sun tea. Do you take sugar or lemon?"

"Lemon."

Jolene went into the small kitchen and opened the refrigerator. As she took out the tea and a lemon, she heard the chair Midge had been sitting in squeak and turned in time to see Midge slip across the room to the table.

She filled two glasses and put a slice of lemon on the side of each before she returned to the living room. Midge was sitting at the table.

"That fan is too noisy," Midge complained. "This is fine here." She took the glass of tea and Jolene joined her at the table, trying not to look again in the direction of her now-open backpack.

She had zipped it closed, hadn't she? But why would Midge open it? Only one person would know about the murder story—the author. And of course Jolene. And the student who was bringing it to her. And maybe the friend of the author.

Jolene groaned inwardly at the thought of how many people might know about the story.

"Aren't you curious about what I brought you?" Midge asked, sounding perturbed. Perturbed because Jolene hadn't thanked her yet? Or because she hadn't found what she'd been looking for in Jolene's backpack?

Pulling the basket toward her, she saw that it was filled with store-bought muffins. In this part of Montana, bringing store-bought anything was almost an insult.

"How thoughtful. Thank you."

Midge gave a slight shrug. "I hadn't welcomed you since you were hired. How are things going?"

"Fine. No problems."

Midge took a drink of her tea, winced and said, "It's bitter. I think you left it out in the sun too long. I've had enough anyway." She shoved the nearly full glass away and rose.

Jolene got up to see her out, but Midge didn't make it to the door before she turned, hands clasped in front of her and said, "I heard you were asking questions about some unpleasant business from years back." She tsked. "You really don't want to concern yourself with that sort of thing. We like our teachers to concentrate on making a pleasant, educational environment for our students. I would suggest you restrict any research projects to the part of our history for which we have pride, such as our early homesteaders."

Jolene was so shocked she couldn't reply at first and then she had to bite her tongue to keep from telling Midge Atkinson what she thought of her suggestion.

Midge's quick smile was more a grimace as she turned abruptly toward the door. "Oh, and I would like my basket back when you've finished with the muffins."

"Of course." As the irritating woman drove away, Jolene closed the door and leaned against it, wondering who in the Whitehorse Sewing Circle had ratted her out.

DULCIE STOPPED AT THE TOP of the stairs and took a shallow breath. The air up here on the second floor of the farmhouse seemed even more foul and stagnant than the floor below. She looked down the hallway toward the front of the house. Four doors stood partially open.

Behind the one closest to her, she saw a broom closet with an ancient vacuum leaning against one wall and a ratty broom.

Stepping lightly, she edged toward the next door. The room was nearly empty except for an old treadle sewing machine sitting against one wall.

Dulcie moved to the next door and peered in. The little girl's room. Someone had painted a blue-and-white ceiling resembling sky and clouds. On the walls around the bed were painted half a dozen angels, complete with wings and cherubic sweet faces. Had the mother painted these?

As Dulcie stepped into the room, she saw that the artist had signed his or her name in the bottom of one corner of the room. M. Atkinson.

The name meant nothing to her. She glanced again at the paintings. A roomful of angels for a little girl named Angel. She tried to picture the little girl who'd lived here. Tomboy or doll-playing princess?

Nothing about the room felt familiar. With a sigh of relief, Dulcie told herself she'd never seen it before. If she'd come to Whitehorse with her parents for whatever reason, then she'd stayed outside this house—outside where she could see the yellow curtains in the second-floor bedroom window and hear the weather vane on the barn.

A small, once-white dresser stood against one wall. She pulled out a drawer. Empty. She tried another. Also empty. How strange that everything else in this house seemed to be just as it had been left twenty-four years ago, except that Angel's clothes were missing. Why take a dead child's clothing?

RUSSELL CALLED THE NUMBER his father had given him, surprised when a girl answered the phone. For a moment, he thought he'd dialed the wrong number.

"Is there a Finnegan Amherst there?"

"My grandfather. Just a moment." The phone dropped but a few moments later a raspy, deep-throated voice asked who was calling.

"Russell Corbett from the Trails West Ranch outside of Whitehorse, Montana."

He heard a soft, dry chuckle. "I wondered when you'd be calling."

"Then you must know what I'm calling about," Russell said, hoping his father and the other ranchers and farmers weren't about to throw their money down a rat hole. The rainmaker definitely *sounded* like someone's grandfather—old grandfather.

"You need a rainmaker," Finnegan Amherst said.

"We need *rain*," Russell corrected.

Again the man chuckled.

"So are you interested?"

The rainmaker sighed. "Let me think about it. If I decide to come up, I'll be there tomorrow. Otherwise I'll call."

With a curse Russell realized that the man had hung up.

"Might as well go waste some more time," he said to himself as he headed for his pickup, sure Dulcie Hughes would drive a hard bargain for her land.

DIRECTLY ACROSS THE HALL from Angel Beaumont's room was the bathroom. Dulcie could make out a large old claw-footed tub against the back wall.

She moved cautiously toward the front bedroom. Through the partially open door, she could see part of the faded yellow curtains billowing in the hot air stealing in through a broken pane.

A chair was positioned by the window, a book lying on the floor, open and facedown and like everything else in the house, covered with dust.

Dulcie hesitated at the threshold to the room. She touched the door, pushing it all the way open. Nothing came scampering out, but she heard the sound of tiny feet overhead and thought of those critters Russell had warned her about.

When she stepped in, she saw the wallpaper and felt a jolt. She *knew* this pattern of old-fashioned tiny yellow flowers. It was so familiar that her knees threatened to buckle under her as she tried to fight the crush of dread mixed with terror.

She *had* been in this room. The room where Laura Beaumont was murdered. Her parents wouldn't have brought her up here. So how was it possible?

Feeling sick, she gripped the doorjamb for a moment until the light-headedness passed.

Dulcie had made a point of not focusing on the high double bed with its antique iron frame. But suddenly she couldn't stop her gaze from going to the soiled mattress.

Cringing, she looked away to see a large chest of drawers against the wall.

As if sleepwalking, she crossed the room and opened the top drawer to find it filled with women's undergarments. The second drawer had more of the same. The third and fourth held shirts and blouses, jeans and slacks.

Someone had taken the child's clothes, but left the mother's?

She opened the closet. Dust-coated dresses hung limp from metal hangers. Shoes were scattered across the closet floor. A closet full of high heels and pretty dresses.

Yellow must have been her favorite color. Just as it was Dulcie's. She closed the closet door, ready to flee as she wished on a ragged breath that she'd never come here.

With a start, she caught movement on the other side of the room. A scream rose in her throat but she quickly tamped it down as she realized what she'd seen. Her own reflection in a cloudy mirror over a vanity on the opposite wall.

The top of the vanity was cluttered with a brush, a mirror, an assortment of bottles and jars, all coated with thick dust.

Dulcie suddenly needed fresh air, even brutally hot air. She started to close the closet door, bumping into the dresser. Something slithered down the wall to the floor.

She stepped back, ready to scream, but stopped when she saw what had fallen. Squatting, she gingerly picked up what appeared to be a snapshot that had fallen from behind the dresser and landed facedown on the floor.

She turned it over and stared into the face of a little girl. A face so like her own, it could have been her twin. Or Dulcie herself.

Chapter Six

From the floor below came a thunk as if something had been knocked over. Startled, Dulcie stuffed the photo in her pocket and looked around for anything she could use to defend herself.

She was thinking about critters when she tiptoed down the hallway toward the top of the stairs. She grabbed the old broom from the small closet and positioned herself on one side of the stairs, ready for anything that came racing up.

A stair creaked under the weight of a heavy boot heel. It must be a pretty large critter, she thought. Russell Corbett? Had he come back to see if she needed protecting? Or maybe to give her more advice?

As the footfalls neared, she clutched the broom in both hands, planning to use it like a bat if necessary. But even as she stepped to the top of the stairs, armed and ready, she was hoping to see Russell Corbett's handsome face looking up at her.

No such luck. This man was barrel big, his face round and beefy, his look murderous. She swallowed back the scream that rose in her throat, tightening her grip on the broom handle, ready to start swinging.

"What the hell do you think you're doing?" the man demanded, stopping halfway up the stairs. His face was enflamed with anger. "You have no business being in this house. You're trespassing and you're damned lucky I haven't called the sheriff."

"You come one step closer and I won't be responsible for what I do with this broom."

They both started at the sound of footfalls behind the man.

"Ben? What are you doing here?" Russell asked from the bottom of the stairs as he looked from the big, angry man to Dulcie and her broom.

"I was just asking this trespasser the same thing," the man said as he shot Dulcie a withering look. "I'm about to take that broom away from her."

"I'd reconsider that if I were you, since you're threatening the owner of this place and could end up in jail yourself," Russell informed him.

Dulcie loosened her grip on the broom, but didn't put it down as the man retreated back down the stairs. She followed after a moment to find both men standing in the living room, looking at her with anything but pleasure.

"He says you own the place?" demanded the man Russell had called Ben. "You have any proof of that?"

"I do."

It took a few moments before the man realized she had no intention of showing it to him.

"And you are…?" she asked.

"Ben Carpenter. I was just driving by."

Russell raised a brow. She could tell he didn't like the man.

Ben scowled at Dulcie. "You thinking of moving in here?"

The question was so ludicrous even Russell seemed to have a hard time keeping a straight face.

"I'm not sure of my plans," she said.

Ben shook his head. "Give it some thought. Your kind don't last long here."

Her *kind?*

Russell tensed, all cordiality gone. "I think you've said quite enough, Ben."

"Yeah?" He looked like he might argue, even throw a few punches, but apparently changed his mind. "I guess I'll just leave the two of you to whatever it is you're doing," he said with a nasty sneer before stomping out the door, angling toward an old pickup parked on the road.

"You just make friends wherever you go," Russell said, shoving back his hat to grin at her.

"It's a knack," she agreed. "Who *is* he?"

"One of your neighbors. He manages a ranch a few miles down the road in the other direction."

"So he wasn't just driving by."

"Nope," Russell said, rubbing his jaw thoughtfully as he looked out the door after Ben.

As he turned to her again, she said with a grin, "So he probably wasn't just driving past like *you* were."

He smiled and glanced around. "You find what you were looking for?"

"Who said I was looking for anything?"

He chuckled at that. "Have you had dinner, what they call supper up here?"

She shook her head. "The kitchen's a mess," she joked.

"I know a place that cooks up a pretty good steak in town. Unless, of course, you're one of those *vegetarians*."

"Do I look like a woman who can't handle her beef?"

"No siree, you look like a woman who can handle

most anything. But what exactly *were* you planning to do with that broom?"

JOLENE WAS SURPRISED and delighted when Tinker Horton called to ask her out. She hadn't expected him back before the weekend.

"I know this is late notice, but I'm in town and I really was hoping you'd be up to having supper with me."

The thought brightened her day instantly. It had been a terrible day and supper out was always a treat.

"I would love to," she said with a laugh as she returned the unread short stories to her backpack again. At the rate things were going she wasn't going to get them read and graded until later tonight.

"Do you mind if we meet in town? I've done all the driving I can stand for one day. I'll make it up to you by taking you to Northern Lights."

"You're on. What time?"

They agreed on a time to meet and Jolene headed for the shower to get ready.

She'd met Thomas "Tinker" Horton her first week in Old Town Whitehorse. They'd run into each other at the Whitehorse Community Center when he'd asked her to dance. Tinker traveled from rodeo to rodeo as a bull rider. She got the feeling he didn't make much money, but that he loved the notoriety since he was famous in this part of the state.

It seemed that he made it back home to Whitehorse more often since they'd met, she thought with a smile.

Tinker was four years older, thirty-three, but he didn't act it. Nor did she see him as a potential boyfriend. They got along fine and seemed to enjoy each other's company. But when he was gone, she didn't miss him and suspected he felt the same way.

Tonight, though, she decided to wear her best dress. It was too fancy for even the Northern Lights, but she was so happy to be getting away from everything for the night, she was going all out.

The dress was the color of autumn leaves. It brought out the reddish highlights in her dark hair. She checked herself in the mirror, pleased. Nothing could ruin this night.

As Jolene went out the door, she grabbed the muffins Midge had brought her. Tinker ate anything when he was on the road. He'd appreciate the muffins and now she'd be able to take Midge's basket back to her. This was working out well.

As she walked toward her car, she noticed that there was something stuck under the windshield wiper on the driver's side.

She plucked a small folded sheet of white paper from beneath her wiper. There was just enough light from the overhead farm light to read the crudely written note.

Watch your step.

"You clean up nice," Russell said when he picked Dulcie up at her motel.

She smiled. "I could say the same of you." And just when she thought he couldn't look more handsome. He wore a pale gray Stetson, a red-checked Western shirt, jeans and boots. While he was dressed much like the first time she'd seen him, there was definitely something different about him tonight.

He looked shy and ill at ease. He didn't date much, she thought, and she found that charming. So what had made him ask *her* out? she wondered, amused.

He opened the passenger-side door of his pickup for her, so chivalrous, and went around to slide behind the wheel. She felt as if she was going to her first prom. It gave her an odd, almost old-fashioned feeling.

Country music came on the radio as he started the truck. She was disappointed when he reached over and turned it off.

Whitehorse was hopping tonight and the Northern Lights restaurant was no exception. Dulcie counted a couple dozen pickups parked along the main street. She could hear more country music coming from one of the bars down the street as she and Russell entered the busy restaurant.

It surprised her a little to realize he'd reserved a table for them. But then Russell Corbett didn't seem like a man who left much to chance.

"So want to tell me what this is really about?" she asked once they were seated and the waitress had taken their orders for two large T-bone steaks, medium rare.

"I wanted a steak?" he said.

She smiled and shook her head.

"I wanted to get to know you better?"

That made her chuckle.

"What if I told you it was a spur-of-the-moment invitation that I regretted the minute I asked?"

She laughed. "That's more like it."

He seemed to relax. "I *am* curious about you."

"How so?"

"I can't figure you out. You're obviously a city girl and yet you've got grit. I couldn't believe it when I saw you with that crowbar. Not many women would have gone into that house."

"Confession? I didn't want to. I almost chickened out."

"Then why put yourself through it? You can see by

looking at that house that it's not worth anything. Any value is in the land."

"I wasn't *appraising* the place," she said, looking into his warm, open, handsome face. "It's hard to explain."

He seemed to settle into his chair as if he had all night.

There was something about him, a peacefulness, a strength, an old-fashioned integrity and honesty that garnered her trust.

"As I told you, I *inherited* the property. Where the problem comes in is that my elderly parents, in the years before they both died, insisted I know everything about their estate. They had wanted to make it as painless for me as possible by gifting me as much as they could over the years."

"They sound like very loving, responsible parents."

"Exactly. So imagine my surprise when this piece of Montana property comes at me from out of left field."

"You like baseball?"

She blinked.

"The baseball analogy? I thought you might be a Cubs fan."

She had to chuckle. "I am. My father took me to many of their games." She could see by Russell's smile that he liked her a little better. Being a fellow Cubs fan was all it took?

"Sorry, I didn't mean to interrupt your story."

"That's just it. There isn't much more to tell. I inherited the property, apparently from Laura Beaumont, via my parents. I'd never heard of her. Then I find out she was murdered and that she had a *daughter*. It brought up the obvious questions. Why hadn't the daughter inherited the property unless she was deceased—or..."

"Or *you* were the daughter?"

She nodded, glad he was tracking her thoughts.

"Is that possible?" he asked.

"Apparently not, since little Angel Beaumont was found drowned in the creek after she went missing following her mother's death. So how did I inherit property at the age of four from a woman I've never heard of? And why didn't my parents ever mention it? All I can figure is that there is a connection between me and Laura Beaumont. But what is it and why would my parents keep this from me?"

He shook his head and waited as if he knew there was more.

Dulcie drew out the photograph and handed it across to him. "To make things worse, I found this in the house today. I looked just like the girl in the photo at that age."

He studied the photo, then her and handed it back. "Is it possible this girl is related to you?"

She shrugged. "I used to have an imaginary friend. I told everyone she was my little sister. I called her Angel." Dulcie looked over at him, her gaze locking with his as she felt a shudder quake through her. "Just another coincidence? Or is it possible that my whole life is a lie?"

JOLENE TRIED TO FORGET about the stupid note she'd found on her car. Midge had probably put it there.

Except it sounded…threatening. But would she have found it threatening if she wasn't secretly getting the murder story?

Midge had warned her not to go digging around in Laura Beaumont's murder. Why would she care unless there was something to find? And what business was it of Midge's what Jolene did?

Jolene thought back to when she'd tried to question

the members of the Whitehorse Sewing Circle. She recalled the way Ella Cavanaugh had looked at Pearl, as
if afraid to say something she shouldn't.

Jolene couldn't believe what she was thinking as she
drove toward Whitehorse. That the whole community
might be involved in keeping a secret about the murder.
Did they know who killed Laura and had been protecting
that person for the past twenty-four years?

That seemed even more far-fetched. Maybe it was
just as Midge had said, an unpleasant part of the area's
history that the community didn't want dug up. So why
didn't Jolene believe that?

Like the books she loved to read, she knew a good
mystery when she found one. She also understood that
in any good mystery there were clues that needed to be
uncovered. In this case, finding those clues meant digging into the murder even further.

Word had gotten out much too quickly in this isolated, small community that she'd been asking about
the murder. Anything more she did would be known
and even possibly jeopardize her job.

But as she hit the outskirts of Whitehorse, she was
thinking about the next segment of the story—and planning to pick up the assignments herself on Thursday
in the hope of finding out where the murder story was
coming from.

What worried her most was why someone had chosen
her to tell their story to—true or not. She couldn't shake
off the feeling that the writer was feeding her information about the murder for a reason other than a critique
of the writing.

But why not give the information to the sheriff if the
author knew something? Unless the story was actually
a confession…

Another thought struck her. What if the author was tired of being part of the conspiracy and had decided to tell an outsider the truth, that outsider being someone safe and trustworthy like, say, the schoolteacher?

Jolene desperately wanted to talk to someone about the murder story and bounce her theories off them. But the moment she saw Tinker's face, she knew she wasn't going to mention it to him.

"Hi, beautiful," he said, brushing her cheek with a kiss. "You look good enough to eat."

She smiled. "I take it the rodeos went well?" He was always in a good mood when he won the bigger purses.

"Well enough to buy you the best meal this side of Miles City."

"You're on, big spender," she said as she took his arm and let him lead her toward the restaurant.

It startled Dulcie when Russell reached across the table and covered her hand.

"I can see this has you upset," he said. "But aren't you jumping to conclusions without any real basis? A lot of kids resemble each other and aren't related."

"Women have a God-given right to jump to conclusions without any basis. Comes with the genes," she joked, hiding how serious this was for her.

He shook his head. "Not you."

"And you base that on…?"

"Being around you a total of five minutes."

She smiled. "Normally, you would be right. But in this case given these feelings I keep having—" She had to swallow the lump in her throat. It was one thing to let her mind run off in this direction, it was another to voice her suspicions.

"What feelings?" he asked as if seeing how upset this had her.

"When I first saw the house, actually when I saw the yellow curtains in the upstairs window, I had this sense of having been there before. In some other areas of the house, I got a horrible feeling of dread, followed almost at once by an irrational fear."

He was studying her openly.

"I heard that Laura Beaumont's daughter might have found her body," Dulcie said, needing desperately to voice her worse fears. "What if she saw the killer?"

She had to take a sip of her wine to steady herself. She hadn't even told Renada, her best friend, and here she was baring her soul to this cowboy she'd just met.

"That's a lot of what-ifs," Russell said.

"There must have been evidence taken from the murder scene," she said after a moment. "If there is any DNA to test…"

"You're that afraid that you're Angel Beaumont?"

"It's the only thing that makes any sense. You understand now why I have to find out the truth one way or the other?"

He squeezed her hand. "I do. But if you're right, then I'm sure your parents had a good reason for not telling you about this, and that it was done out of love."

Tears burned her eyes at his kindness and she had to look away not to cry. A young couple had just come in the door. The cowboy was good-looking in a cocky, got-it-all-going-on kind of way. But it was the woman who caught Dulcie's eye. She was tall and pretty with a mane of chestnut hair. There was something familiar about her…

"There has to be a simple explanation that will clear this whole thing up."

"Thank you," Dulcie said to Russell as she turned

back to him and pulled herself together. "I just needed to say all of that out loud. I feel better."

He grinned at her. "I'm glad I could help."

Their salads arrived just then and they lost themselves in the food and talking about other things. She asked about Texas and Whitehorse. He asked about Chicago and the Cubs games.

The evening passed in a pleasant blur of good food and equally good conversation. There was a lot more to Russell Corbett than met the eye—and in his case, that was saying a lot.

As they were leaving, she again noticed the young woman whom she'd seen with the cocky cowboy. As Dulcie passed their table on the way out of the restaurant, the woman looked up, a smile coming automatically to her lips, then a look of recognition and surprise.

That's when it came to Dulcie why the woman had looked so familiar. She was the one Dulcie had run into coming out of the newspaper office—the one who'd dropped the copy of the article about the murder investigation.

What surprised Dulcie was the fear in the young woman's face at seeing her again.

Chapter Seven

Russell noticed the change in Dulcie as they were leaving the restaurant. "Anything wrong?"

"That young couple we passed as we were leaving, do you know them?"

He'd seen Dulcie hesitate at that last table. "That's Tinker. You probably don't follow rodeo. Thomas 'Tinker' Horton's a pretty famous bull rider in these parts."

"I was more interested in the woman with him," Dulcie said, surprising him. Most women would have been more interested in Tinker.

"That's the new schoolteacher in Old Town Whitehorse, Jolene Stevens."

"Not that tiny school I saw next to the community center?"

He grinned at her obvious surprise as he opened his truck door for her. "It's your old-fashioned one-room schoolhouse. I think I heard she has five students this year, grades three through eight."

"I had no idea," Dulcie said as he slid behind the wheel. "I thought one-room schools were a thing of the past. So she drives to and from Whitehorse every day?"

"The community provides her with a house in Old

Town. It's that cute little white one past the center and down the hill a ways. Why all the questions about the schoolteacher?"

Dulcie shrugged. "I ran into her the other day in Whitehorse. I was just curious who she was."

He cut his eyes to her, knowing there was more to it.

She gave him an innocent look. "What else could it be?"

His question exactly. Dulcie looked out the side window as they drove to the motel, clearly not going to tell him what her real interest was in Jolene Stevens.

"You never told me what you do," he said as he pulled up in front of her motel room.

"Do?"

"For work. You do work, don't you?"

"Why? You think I have so much money I don't have to work?"

"I've heard tell of such a thing." He hadn't had to work for financial reasons his entire life, thanks to the Corbett wealth, but he thought everyone needed a job, a goal, something to do.

"I owned a business with a friend. We just sold it. I'm looking around for something else to keep me out of trouble."

"No small order that," he said as he got out to open her door. "I enjoyed dinner, especially watching you eat that steak. You are a woman after my own heart," he said as she stepped out into the starlight.

"Oh?" She cocked her head, grinning at him.

"You aren't flirting with me, are you?"

Her soft laugh was all music. "Would that be so bad?"

No, he thought, unless he was foolish enough to lose

his heart to this city girl. But there was no chance of that. Especially if he didn't make the mistake of kissing her under the starlight.

Damn, but she *was* asking for it though.

TINKER GREW QUIET AS HE walked Jolene to her car. She hadn't been able to get a word in edgewise all during dinner. Tinker did love to talk about himself.

But with the night winding down, she thought this might be the perfect time to ask if he remembered the murder. "So you've lived here in Whitehorse your whole life."

"I don't like to think about it," Tinker joked as he leaned against her car and grinned at her. "I just come home now to see you."

"You don't have family here?" she asked, surprised.

"My mom," he said. "She remarried when I was little. My stepfather and I don't get along. But she loves the bastard so…" He straightened, clearly not wanting to talk about it.

"Do you remember a murder twenty-four years ago outside of Old Town Whitehorse?" she blurted out.

Tinker looked surprised, then annoyed. "Why ask me?"

She wished she hadn't. For some reason the question had ruined Tinker's good mood. "It's nothing. Just something I was curious about."

He was shaking his head, clearly angry. "That's a damned odd thing to be curious about."

"It's just that I thought you might have known the daughter, Angel Beaumont. She would have been younger than you…"

"Did someone tell you I knew her?" he demanded.

"No, I just—"

"Just heard that my stepfather was the ranch manager on the Atkinson place across the creek," he said angrily. "Well, he got fired because of Laura Beaumont, okay? We had to move to a run-down old place and my mother…" He shook his head, clearly agitated now. "I don't know what some busybodies have been telling you—"

"No one's been telling me anything."

He glared at her. "Why are you digging up this old crap after all this time?"

She shook her head, at a loss since she couldn't tell him about the murder story, especially now. "I'm sorry. I—"

"Oh, that's right, you've got Mace in your class."

Mace Carpenter? Now she really was confused. "Wait a minute, Ben Carpenter is your stepfather?"

"As if you didn't know that."

"I didn't. I swear." Ronda Carpenter was Tinker's mother?

He looked away and when his gaze returned to her, there was a coldness to it. "I knew Angel, okay? I felt sorry for her. Her mother was a tramp who didn't pay any attention to her. I'd already lived through my mother's divorce and her remarrying Ben. I could relate so I tried to watch out for the kid."

She didn't know what to say. Tinker was the friend from the murder story?

"Angel was a sweet little girl. She didn't stand a chance though. I wasn't surprised when her mother got herself murdered and Angel…" He shook his head again. "I don't like talking about any of this."

"I'm sorry. I really had no idea." She should have, though, given how small the community was.

He glanced at his watch. "I've got to go."

"Thanks for supper."

"Sure." He started to step away, but turned back. "I wouldn't go talking to anyone else about this if I were you. People around here don't like you digging up bad memories." He left her standing beside her car, feeling awful for spoiling their evening out.

But at least now she knew. Tinker had to be the friend in the murder story. He would have been nine, Angel four or five. Why else would he have been so upset?

Still she couldn't help but feel strange about him telling her not to talk to anyone else about it.

First the Whitehorse Sewing Circle, then Midge, now Tinker. Her conspiracy theory raised its ugly head again. Who were they all trying to protect?

RUSSELL WALKED DULCIE to her motel-room door under a canopy of starlight and just a sliver of a moon. There was no one around, the hot night breathlessly silent.

She made the mistake of looking over at him. Their gazes locked. "Thank you, Russell, for—"

He reached for her, bunching a handful of her wild mane at her nape in his fist as he pulled her to him. Her brown eyes fired with a heat he hadn't seen for a long time—even longer, felt.

Her lips parted. He dropped his mouth over hers, felt the soft remnants of a smile disappear as he kissed her—and she kissed him back.

He encircled her with his arms, holding her as the kiss ended. Slowly, he drew back to look into her eyes. Her gaze was as dark as the night. It stirred a fire in him, sparking a yearning that had lain dormant far too long.

If only it had been with some other woman…*any* other woman.

He let go of her and started to open his mouth to speak.

"If you say you're sorry for kissing me so help me I'll slug you," Dulcie said, narrowing her eyes at him.

He laughed because that's exactly what he'd been about to do. He brushed a lock of her hair back from her cheek with his thumb. "What will you do now?"

"Go to bed."

"No, I mean—"

"I know what you mean." She looked up toward the heavens. "I never make decisions at night, especially after a big steak and—" she lowered her gaze to him "—an amazing kiss. Can't trust your judgment at times like that."

He smiled. "You're a smart woman."

"Aren't I, though? Good night, Russ. Sweet dreams." She turned and went inside.

He stood smiling after her, then walked to his truck. It wasn't until he was almost to the ranch that he realized he hadn't made an offer on her land. He hadn't even broached the subject.

But then it wasn't good to make a decision after a big steak and an amazing kiss, now, was it?

WHEN JOLENE STARTED toward school the next morning, she noticed a pickup parked out front and feared there was a problem with one of her students.

The schoolhouse door was propped open. As she approached it, she wondered who in the community had a key besides her.

Titus Cavanaugh was sitting behind her desk, leaning back, eyes closed. For a moment she thought he was asleep.

Titus, a large, white-haired man with a powerful voice

and a strong handshake, was pretty much in charge of everything in Old Town Whitehorse.

He opened his eyes as she approached and she saw that he hadn't been sleeping. "Hello." He smiled broadly. "I just came by before class to see how you were doing."

"Fine, I think," she said, sliding into one of her students' chairs.

"Good." He crossed his arms and leaned over her desk to look at her. "No trouble with that Carpenter boy?"

She shook her head. "Should I be having trouble with him?"

Titus laughed. "The last teacher found him…temperamental."

Jolene debated how much to say. "I did wonder if he might not have some issues at home."

"Indeed," Titus said with a nod of his head. "How about his father? The last teacher also had trouble with him."

"Ben stopped by yesterday to ask how his son was doing in school. I told him Mace was doing fine."

"Good." Titus rose to his feet. "I just wanted to make sure you weren't having any problems. Ben can be kind of a bully. If you have any trouble with him, you let me know." His blue eyes glinted as he smiled. "It sounds as if you're doing a fine job. Oh, by the way, the door was open when I arrived."

"I locked it last night. At least I would have sworn I did." Jolene worried that she'd been distracted and might *not* have locked it.

"I suppose there could be some keys floating around from former teachers," he said. "Don't worry about it. No harm done. It's not like there is much to steal."

She walked Titus out. Back at her desk, she noticed

that one of the drawers was partially open. Had she left it like that?

Opening the drawer, she glanced at the short stories she'd already read and graded. Someone had gone through the stack.

WHEN DULCIE OPENED THE door to her motel room the next morning, she found Russell Corbett leaning against his pickup, waiting for her. She was instantly reminded of their kiss and felt a pleasurable warmth flow through her bloodstream.

"How do you feel about breakfast?"

She smiled, surprised how glad she was to see him. Last night, she hadn't told him why she was asking questions about the schoolteacher because she'd seen how scared the teacher had been at seeing her again. Whatever it was about, she felt she needed to keep the teacher's secret.

Nor was she going to talk about her problems. She only had a few more days here and she wanted them to be pleasant. Russell Corbett made them pleasant.

"I'm *for* breakfast."

"Good, because I worked up an appetite standing around out here," he said, opening her door.

"You could have just knocked on my door," she said as she slipped into the passenger seat.

"And disturb your sleep? I couldn't chance that you're one of those people who's crabby if she doesn't get enough sleep," he said, starting the engine.

She smiled to herself as she studied him, his big hands on the wheel, and with that almost arrogant confidence about him that drew her in spite of herself.

"Okay," she said later, after she'd put away a large slice of ham, two eggs, hash browns and toast. "Let's hear it."

"Hear what?"

"Two meals, compliments and all this chivalry? What's this about?"

"I don't know what you mean."

"Sure you do. This is not how you spend your mornings *or* your evenings." She reached for his hand, turning it over to expose the thick callouses. "This time of the morning you'd be working if it wasn't for me. So why aren't you? I saw the look on your face. You were upset to see the way I was dressed this morning. If this is about keeping me away from that house—"

"Now that you mention it," he said, frowning as he pulled his hand back. "I don't like the idea of you going back there by yourself."

"That's sweet, but what does your boss say about you missing work to babysit me?"

He hesitated just a little too long.

"What?"

"I wasn't completely honest with you about my job. Trails West Ranch is a family-owned operation."

"And you're one of the family." She couldn't be angry with him, given that she hadn't originally been completely honest about the businesses she'd started with Renada.

"We're interested in buying your property if you decide to sell it."

"So that's it." What had she thought? That he might be interested in *her?*

"Not entirely," he said, but she was already on her feet.

"You're more than welcome to make an offer when I sell the land. I'll let you know. Thanks for breakfast. No, please, stay and enjoy your coffee. I'd prefer to walk."

"Dulcie—"

The door slammed behind her. "Handled that well," she muttered under her breath, angry with herself for making it so obvious how much that had hurt.

JOLENE COLLECTED THE short-story assignments herself, counting them as she went. She hadn't gotten much sleep last night. Her thoughts kept circling around her conspiracy theory about Laura Beaumont's murder.

Nor did it help to find Titus waiting for her this morning after someone had been in the schoolhouse and gone through the drawer with the stories in it.

When Jolene had gotten back to Old Town Whitehorse last night, she'd been spooked remembering the note she'd found earlier that night on her windshield. She'd gone through her small house, checking all the windows and doors to make sure they were locked and the closets were free of any intruders.

It had felt silly and yet she couldn't shake the feeling that all this was about more than some aspiring author using her for a free critique of his or her work.

This morning she'd finally admitted her worst fear— that Laura Beaumont's killer had resurfaced, if he'd ever left to begin with, and now he was writing his story just for her.

Suddenly she stopped in the middle of her classroom and counted the short-story assignments she'd collected. There were only *five*.

She counted them again. Just as she'd feared, the murder story wasn't among them.

"Don't you want that one?" asked her third-grader, Amy Brooks.

Jolene turned and looked at the girl. Amy was pointing at the corner of a table in the back of the classroom where stapled-together papers were lying on it, facedown.

"Does anyone know who left this here?" she asked her class, glancing at each of the five. Blank faces stared back at her. "Has it been here every time you collected the stories?" she asked her students.

Amy nodded. "Isn't it from your other student?"

"My *other* student?" Jolene repeated.

"Don't you have one who can't come to class and sends things in?" she asked. "You know, like an online student?"

"A ghost student," her fifth-grader brother, Thad, said with a laugh.

"Yeah, *ooooooo*," Luke chimed in. "Ghosts."

"All right, that's enough. It's Thursday so that means we have one more day of writing the middle of the story and then you will have the weekend to complete the end."

There was a groan from the two fifth-graders.

"You're about to wind up your story. What else do you need to tell your reader before the ending? That's what you should think about when you write tonight."

She picked up the pages from the small desk at the back and turned them over. More of the murder story. She felt her pulse quicken with both relief—and dread. Monday it would end.

But how?

The searing wind was a demon moving over the lifeless land. With no sign of rain in the forecast, the tension had grown until it was like a wire strung too tightly. Everyone waited, knowing it was just a matter of time before something snapped.

Among the farmers and ranchers there was a growing sense of panic. The men talked among themselves in quiet desperation. The women tried to keep the children from irritating their fathers.

A silent fear had settled in. If it didn't rain soon, there would be no crops, no money. They had been through hard times before, but this time might be the final straw that broke the camel's back.

While she fanned herself and watched the road or slogged through chores that couldn't be put off, the rest of the community hung on each blistering breath and prayed and cursed and worried.

Not that she was immune to the growing strain in the country and people around her. She was part of it, this pressure that pushed some to the edge, for she had grown bored and restless. Her lover had to sense it and feel another kind of quiet desperation.

The hottest day that spring, she lifted her head as if sniffing the air. An old pickup clattered up the road, the metal pipes he carried in the back humming like a siren call. Did he glimpse her standing at her bedroom window, lifting her long, richly burnished hair from her slim neck?

Or did he first see her on her porch scantily dressed one night as she searched for a cool breeze?

In the days that followed when he tried to work his magic in the pasture near her farmhouse, he watched both the sky and the woman.

How different things might have been if the rainmaker had resisted her. Or if the rain hadn't come too late.

How lucky though that the little girl had a friend she met at the creek. He was older, one of those lost souls who had seen too much in his young life and expected to see much worse before it was over.

He liked the girl, felt protective of her. He watched the farmhouse and he knew what went on there. That's why on that horribly hot day he lured the little girl away from the house. Not to help the killer, but to save his friend.

If only he could have kept her from going back to the house, from finding her mother like that, from seeing the killer—and the killer seeing her.

"I TAKE IT YOU DIDN'T HAVE any better luck this morning than you did last night?" Grayson Corbett asked as Russell stalked into the main house, scowling.

"That woman is impossible," he muttered as he poured himself a cup of coffee from the carafe behind the bar.

Kate was smiling at him. "How was supper at Northern Lights?"

"Fine." He didn't want to talk about his date. "She's going back over to the house today. If she doesn't break her fool neck, maybe I'll go over and try to talk some sense into her."

"You might just want to keep it strictly business," Grayson suggested.

"Or you might want to ask her out again," Kate said.

Russell shook his head. "I doubt either will do me any good. Maybe I should just leave it to you," he said to his father. "You might have better luck with her."

Grayson shook his head. "Kate's probably right. A woman likes to be courted—even in business."

"Flowers are always a nice gesture," Kate suggested.

Russell scoffed inwardly at that. He'd already done too much courtin' of Dulcie Hughes when he'd kissed her last night in front of her motel room.

No wonder she'd gotten angry this morning at breakfast. She thought that kiss was about getting her land when her property had been the last thing on his mind.

"I've got work to do," Russell said. "I'll go over later and see what I can do to rectify things."

"It's no big deal if we don't get the property," Grayson said. "I understand if you want to forget it."

What he wanted to forget was Dulcie Hughes.

"Any word from that rainmaker?" his father asked.

"No. He said he'd come on up here or he'd call. He hasn't called. I'll get back to him."

Russell tried the rainmaker and got his voice mail. He left a message. As he was driving past the Atkinson place, he swung in. John Atkinson owned that property behind Laura Beaumont's place at the time of the murder. If Russell could find out something for Dulcie, he might be able to help her solve this mystery so she could get back to Chicago and he could get back to work and get her off his mind.

It had nothing to do with getting back into her good graces. She'd just think it was about buying her land and get mad again anyhow.

DULCIE DUCKED INTO THE newspaper office since she was walking past it anyway. It didn't take long to find out what year Jolene Stevens had been looking at and deduce which murder the schoolteacher had made copies of. Why would a schoolteacher be interested in Laura Beaumont's murder?

As Dulcie went through the same stories Jolene had, she noticed something odd. There was no mention of Laura Beaumont's past. No mention of Angel's father. No obit with Laura's maiden name or any background.

Leaving the newspaper, she drove out of town more convinced than before that something was very odd about all of this. Leaves scuttled across the dusty street, propelled by the blistering, dried-out wind. It was early in the morning and yet the temperature was already in the seventies.

She had stopped for gas at Packys on the way out of town, all unpleasant thoughts of Russell Corbett disappearing as she felt the tension growing in the community. It was as if a spark could set off the locals, just as it could ignite the tinder-dry grasses outside.

The talk everywhere was of the need for rain.

Dulcie found herself caught up in it, anxious and nervous and expectant. She watched the sky for any sign of relief and silently prayed for the heavens to open up and douse them all in reviving moisture that would save not only the crops, but also the peace.

The feeling that she was perched on a powder keg about to blow grew stronger as she pulled past her cut barbed-wire gate lying in the dry grass and parked in front of the old farmhouse.

This empathy she felt for the ranch and farm people surprised her. Growing up in Chicago, she couldn't have been farther from the land and her food source. Here though, she felt as if she were a part of it. Or possibly had been.

You aren't Angel Beaumont.

Wasn't she? she thought as she looked up at the second-floor window and saw the yellow curtains. What felt like a memory nudged her, but refused to come into focus. She was a part of something here and damned if she wasn't going to find out what.

Opening the car door, she stepped out and moved through the tall weeds toward the house—ever vigilant of rattlesnakes.

Hurriedly she climbed the steps, glad to be where she

could see what might be next to her. When she reached the front door, though, she paused.

Yesterday she'd locked the front door as they'd left. She remembered testing it, standing on the porch with Russell. It *had* been locked.

But now as she reached for her key, she saw that the door was slightly ajar. Goose bumps spread over her flesh even in the breathless heat. Her blood pounded in her ears and yet past it she could hear the annoying weather vane moving restlessly in the searing wind.

A new sound set her teeth on edge. The rhythmic clinking of metal on metal coming from behind the house.

Dulcie stepped to the edge of the porch and looked toward the creek and the property beyond her own. Through the branches of the cottonwoods, she could see a man with a sledgehammer, pounding what looked like pipe into the ground on the other side of the creek.

He stopped as if sensing her watching him and looked in her direction. She couldn't see his face under the dark hat he wore, but she could feel his hard, staring eyes on her, his gaze hotter than the spring day.

She stepped back quickly, feeling strangely violated. How was it possible she could feel both hatred and lust, fear and shock and pain in a look?

She knew what Renada would say. This place was making her imagination run wild. Dulcie shook her head at her own foolishness but was thankful when the man resumed his banging.

Just the thought of Renada made her too aware that she hadn't called her friend. Nor had she answered the messages Renada had left. She promised herself she would call her tonight, if only to let her know she was all right.

She knew why she hadn't called and told her about

what had been going on. Renada would be on the next plane out and Dulcie would have loved nothing better. But it would mean taking Renada away from her design classes and something she'd wanted for far too long.

Walking to the front of the house again, Dulcie took a breath and, holding it, flung open the door. It was impossible to tell if there were any new tracks in the dust.

She stepped in, leaving the door open, and moved cautiously toward the kitchen in the back. She hadn't taken two steps when the front door slammed with a loud bang.

She jumped, heart leaping to her throat. Something stirred the air around her. Wind like a blast furnace. Moving toward the source, she found the back door wide-open. Hadn't it been boarded up like the front door? She'd never checked.

Dulcie closed and locked it, using the dead bolt. Then she stood, listening. No sound came from upstairs. But she couldn't convince herself that she wasn't alone in the house until she went upstairs and checked.

She listened again, thankful when she heard the man she'd seen driving pile still working. When she listened really hard, she could hear the creak and groan of the weather vane, but no sound coming from inside the house.

What was she doing here? What more did she hope to find? She wished she knew as she cautiously climbed the stairs, drawn to the front bedroom.

At the doorway, she watched the wind breathing the yellow curtains in and out. She caught a scent on the air, faint but so seductive, it drew her into the room. Yesterday, she'd seen the assortment of bottles thick with dust atop of the vanity.

Now she saw that someone had moved them, leaving tracks in the dust. Avoiding looking in the cloudy mirror, she spotted a perfume bottle, the dust smudged.

Carefully she picked it up, that faint scent she'd caught earlier tempting her. Opening the bottle, she took a whiff. Her throat closed, eyes brimming with tears as she dropped the perfume onto the vanity and stumbled back, her hand clamped over her mouth to keep from crying out.

In the mirror, she saw herself again, saw her terror, and fled the room to stand in the hallway. While the yellow curtains and the sound of the weather vane in the wind had jarred some memory, the scent of Laura Beaumont's perfume had struck a chord so deep in her that it felt as if the very foundation she stood on was crumbling beneath her.

Dulcie slid down the wall to the dusty floor and dropped her face into her hands as her heart thudded wildly and she tried to catch her breath. The scent of Laura Beaumont's perfume was inextricably linked in her mind with that of a crying, terrified little girl—and blood, lots and lots of blood.

Chapter Eight

Arctic-cold air-conditioning blasted Russell as John Atkinson opened the door of the ranch house.

"Russell?" John said, seeming surprised to see him. John Atkinson was a contemporary of Russell's father, a large man in his early sixties with a thick head of salt-and-pepper hair and a weathered face.

"Sorry to drop in without calling, John."

"No, come in. Midge just made a fresh pot." This was rural Montana where a pot of coffee was always on and drop-in visitors were always welcome.

The house had recently been remodeled with all new furnishings that Russell suspected had to do more with Midge's tastes than John's, including the hand-painted flowery borders in every room.

Russell led him into the large ranch kitchen and offered him a chair at the table. While John filled two mugs with coffee, Russell glanced out the window at the view of the Larb Hills etched against the skyline.

John and Midge still had several ranches to the south, but had moved closer to town in the past couple of years. Unlike other ranchers who turned the place over to their grown sons or daughters and son-in-laws, John and Midge had never had children, so his ranches were leased.

"I heard you called in a rainmaker," John said, hand-ing Russell one of the mugs filled with coffee before joining him at the table.

"Finnegan Amherst."

John's head came up with a jerk. He let out a curse, something unusual for John.

"He's the same one that was used some twenty years before. He did make rain the last time, didn't he?"

John waved a hand through the air. "I'm just surprised he's still alive."

An odd thing to say, given that the rainmaker was supposedly younger than John himself.

"Was he in ill health?" Russell had to ask when John didn't say more.

"No, no, I just thought someone would have shot him by now. Or strung him up."

Russell was confused and said as much.

John took a sip of his coffee as if he'd said too much already. "It's his way with women, other men's women."

"Finnegan is a ladies' man?" Russell said with a laugh, remembering the man's deep, raspy voice. "I doubt he is anymore. He sounded on the phone as if he was ninety."

"Really? He's closer to fifty now, I'd say. Making rain must have aged the man."

John's sarcasm and obvious dislike of the rainmaker confused Russell. Was it possible Finnegan Amherst had gone after Midge?

The idea made him scoff. Midge Atkinson wasn't the type of woman that attracted men. There was something too brittle about her. Ah, hell, the woman was a bitch, plain and simple.

"So when is he coming?" John asked.

"Good question. I'm waiting to hear from him."

Russell glanced at his watch and remembered why he'd stopped by.

"I don't know if you've heard, but the owner of the old Beaumont place is in town. She's interested in finding out more about the murder."

All the blood drained from John's face. His coffee mug clattered to the table, coffee spilling everywhere.

John shoved back his chair and hurried into the kitchen to grab some paper towels.

Russell righted the coffee mug. "I take it you remember the murder. I guessed you would, since you had the ranch behind the place," he said as John sopped up the coffee. "You knew Laura Beaumont then?"

Russell hadn't heard Midge Atkinson enter the kitchen until he heard her sharp, low cry behind him. He turned to see her ashen face and the way she looked at her husband.

"I spilt a little coffee. No big deal," John said as she rushed over to snatch the sodden paper towels from him, clearly furious. But was it over spilled coffee or what she'd heard when she'd entered the room?

"I was just asking about Laura Beaumont," Russell said.

"I heard," Midge snapped. "Don't you men have some work to do?"

Russell finished his coffee quickly as she reached for his mug. Taking it from him, she returned to the kitchen and turned on the water in the sink.

He glanced over at John, who shook his head as if to say, "Let it go." As she started to wash out the mugs, he saw her grip the edge of the sink as if hanging on for dear life.

"I've got some things to pick up in town," John called to his wife and motioned for Russell to follow him outside.

"She doesn't like talking about Laura's death," John said once they were out by their trucks. "So I'd really appreciate it if you didn't mention it again."

"Sure," Russell said, wondering if that was all there was to it. But before he could ask why, John ended the conversation by heading to his pickup.

DULCIE SLOWLY BECAME aware of her surroundings. As she lifted her head from her hands, her whole body tensed. Listening, she heard…nothing. The banging on the other side of the creek had stopped. Had the wind died down, as well? She couldn't hear the weather vane.

Her gaze shot down the hall toward the window and the slack, unmoving yellow curtains. No wind. No sound. It was as if she'd suddenly gone deaf.

Get out of the house! Now!

Irrational panic filled her. She shot to her feet, teetering for a moment at the top of the stairs as she looked down into the dim darkness below her. Her feet faltered, but only for a moment as she rushed down the steps.

She only had two steps to go. She'd already taken them in her mind, had already seen herself grasp the doorknob, turn it and fling the door wide, bolting out into the heat and sunlight.

The man appeared at the bottom of the stairs as if materializing out of nothing.

Her scream was bloodcurdling as she grabbed for the stair railing in an attempt to keep from crashing into him. Her fingers slipped on the dusty rail, and finding no purchase, she fell the last two steps, slamming into him.

He looked so fragile, she'd thought the two of them would fall to the floor. Tall and thin, dressed all in black, including his felt hat, it surprised her at how solid he felt, how strong.

His fingers bit into her shoulders as he grabbed her. She fought to free herself and heard him swear as he righted her, holding her away from him, staring into her face.

Dulcie stared back, flinching at what she saw under the soft brim of his beat-up hat—a gaunt face stretched over hard angles and startling dark eyes that shone with something so black it was like falling into a bottomless pit.

She jerked back, repelled by the man, and found her voice. "What are you doing in my house?"

"*Your* house?" The sound of him surprised her as much as the sight of him. A rasp of a voice, well-deep and just as cold.

"*My* house," she repeated, screwing up her courage. "You're trespassing and you know what they do to trespassers up here."

His laugh was hollow, the shine in his eyes hypnotic.

"Get out!" she ordered, her voice spiraling with her fear. "Get out or I'm going to call the police."

His smile showed shockingly uniform white teeth and for a moment she glimpsed what he must have looked like when he was younger.

Her breath caught. As she staggered backward, she threw her hand up as if to ward him off. His hand shot out, brushed her sleeve. Her scream was a shrill cry of raw terror.

"DULCIE? DULCIE!" Russell burst through the front door, stopping short as she shoved past a tall, thin man dressed all in black and ran into his arms.

Russell held her to him and demanded of the man, "Who the hell are you?"

"I'm afraid I frightened her," the man said in a raspy, deep voice that Russell recognized at once. The man turned to face him, giving a slight courtly bow without removing his hat. "Finnegan Amherst, at your service. And you are…?"

"Russell Corbett."

"Ah, the rancher who called requesting my talents. I have already begun my work."

So he *had* shown up. "I hope you aren't planning to make rain inside this ranch house," Russell snapped.

The rainmaker chuckled, a sound like dead, rustling leaves.

He could still feel Dulcie trembling and knew how much it took to scare this woman. What had this man done to her?

"Again, I am sorry if I frightened you, miss." He tipped his hat to Dulcie. "I've set up across the creek. The same place I did last time with much success." His gaze raked over Dulcie, making her shiver again before he left them, closing the door behind him.

"Are you all right?" Russell asked, looking into Dulcie's brown eyes. His fingers brushed back her hair.

She nodded, her eyes locking with his as she held tight to him. Her eyes filled, her full lower lip trembling.

"You're all right," he whispered as he traced a thumb over her lower lip. Her lips parted, the tip of her tongue brushing his rough skin.

DULCIE HEARD HIS GROAN and pressed her body to his. His arm dragged her to him. His mouth came down hard on hers. She gasped as she felt the tip of his tongue tease the inside of her lower lip.

Her breasts, crushed against his hard chest, ached and

as her arms encircled his neck, she felt him lift her from the floor.

She hung on, his mouth never leaving hers, as he backed her up against the wall at the bottom of the stairs, holding her there with his body as his fingers opened her shirt, slipping inside to cup her full, round breast in his warm palm.

She cried out softly, her head lolling back as his thumb found the hardened tip of her nipple. Her arms slipped from around his neck to grasp the front of his Western shirt and pull, the snaps coming undone to reveal his smooth, tanned flesh and the dark trail of fine hair that disappeared in a V into the waist of his jeans.

"Dulcie," he said on a ragged breath.

She closed her eyes as she felt him bare her breasts to his mouth, to his hands, and squirmed against him, wanting him like she'd never wanted any other man.

She opened her eyes and reached for his belt. His mouth came down on hers again as he lifted her higher and worked her canvas pants down. She felt the heat and hardness of him and nothing on earth could have kept her from fulfilling this desire burning in her as he pulled back to look into her eyes.

She reached for him, rocking against his hips, as he took her to the edge of climax and then even higher before quenching her aching need.

RUSSELL HELD HER AGAINST the wall and tried to catch his breath. They were both covered in sweat, their bodies glistening. He slowly lowered her feet to the floor.

"I'm sorry. That wasn't the way I…" His voice trailed off as he realized what he'd been about to say. *That wasn't the way I envisioned making love to you.*

She laughed softly. "Oh. And what *had* you planned?"

He couldn't help but smile. "A bed?"

She shook her head as she slowly began to button her blouse, her brown-eyed gaze locked on his. "I wouldn't have had our first time be any other way. I wanted you as much as you wanted me."

"I doubt that." Their *first* time? He told himself there wouldn't be a second. He could see that she wasn't taking this as seriously as he was. Hell, the woman wasn't taking any of this as seriously as he thought she should. Just being in this house was dangerous. Investigating an unsolved murder could be deadly.

"I know you drove out here to scold me," she said as she dressed.

He couldn't help himself. He leaned toward her and gently kissed her. "I want you to be safe."

"I know." She cupped his face in her hands and, smiling, brushed a kiss over his lips before letting go.

He stepped back, determined that if they ever made love again, it wouldn't be in this old house against a wall and it would be for the right reasons. It wouldn't be lust or fear.

He could hear the rainmaker driving his metal pipes into the ground again. He could see that Dulcie was listening, as well. "What did that man want with you?"

"Nothing," she said as she hugged herself, rubbing her arms with her hands even though they were both perspiring in the heat of the closed-up house. "Nothing."

"He had to have wanted *something*. I saw the look on your face. Dulcie—"

"I'm fine. I'm sorry I scared you."

"Scared *me?* It's you I'm concerned about. That man

is going to be working just across the creek from you. If he touched you or threatened you—"

"I told you, he didn't *do* anything. He just…startled me, that's all, and I overreacted."

She was lying and for the life of him he couldn't imagine why. What would have happened if he hadn't come along when he did? Yesterday it had been Ben Carpenter. Today that damned rainmaker.

Worse, Russell had made love with her and complicated things even more. He wanted to cross the creek and pummel the truth out of that old man, but he had a feeling he'd get the same answer from him.

"That man," she asked. "What kind of work is he doing across the creek?"

"He's a rainmaker."

"You hired him to make *rain?*"

Russell wasn't in the mood to debate this and said as much. He had enough doubts of his own.

She must have seen that he was angry with her as he shoved back his hat and prepared to leave, because she didn't argue the issue. "He said he was here before."

He studied her for a long moment. "Twenty-four years ago." He saw her expression and felt the import of his words on her.

The last time the rainmaker had been here would have been that hot, deadly dry spring when Laura Beaumont was murdered.

THE SCHOOL DAY SEEMED to drag. During recess, Jolene sat in the shade and read the short stories, but her mind wandered.

When the time came to dismiss the students, she was relieved. Monday the school term would end. Since she'd been hired for the coming year as well, she would be allowed to live in the small house down the road for the summer.

She'd been looking forward to the time to read and explore the area. But the heat this spring had curbed her enthusiasm. That and the murder story.

No wonder she felt restless. Tomorrow was Friday. There was only one more segment of the short story. Then the ending on Monday. Would Friday's be waiting for her on the corner of that used desk in the morning when she opened the classroom?

Or would the killer?

She shivered at the thought.

"See you all in the morning. Don't forget," she said as she watched her students noisily preparing to leave. "Keep working on your stories."

She watched from the window as they loaded onto the bus or climbed into waiting pickups and SUVs, then began to gather her belongings, anxious to get home.

At the sound of footfalls, she looked up to find a woman standing in the doorway, looking around as if she'd never seen a one-room schoolhouse before.

"Can I help you?" The woman was studying the birth-day wall, where everyone had posted their upcoming birthdays, hers included, complete with photographs.

As the woman turned, Jolene recognized her. It was the woman she'd bumped into on the street that day outside the newspaper office. The same woman she'd seen at dinner last night at Northern Lights.

"Jolene Stevens?" the woman asked. "I'm Dulcie Hughes. Do you have a minute?"

THE TEACHER'S HAND WAS ice-cold as Dulcie shook it.

"What is this about?"

"Laura Beaumont's murder." Dulcie saw the young

woman's surprise. "Don't bother to tell me you don't know who I'm talking about. I saw the copy of the newspaper article you dropped on the street that day. I checked at the newspaper office and found out which stories you copied."

"I don't understand why—"

"I recently inherited Laura Beaumont's house. Is there somewhere we could talk about this privately?"

Jolene Stevens seemed to hesitate, but only for a moment. "Let's go to my place." She pointed down the dirt street to a cute little cottage. "Just let me lock up the school."

Dulcie waited in the car with the air-conditioning running. She had tried to pull herself together after Russell had left her at the farmhouse. He'd been angry and she couldn't blame him. They'd shared an intimacy that a man like him didn't take lightly. Nor did she, even though she'd let him believe she had.

Even now she couldn't regret what happened, but she also couldn't let it happen again. She'd gotten too close to Russell Corbett.

He'd realized that as well and that was one reason he was so upset with her. He knew she was keeping things from him. But explaining what had happened between her and the rainmaker before Russell had burst in was impossible.

She still didn't understand it herself.

After he'd left, she'd thought about going upstairs to do more digging. She'd already found one photograph. There had to be more since nothing seemed to have been taken but the child's clothing. Wasn't it possible there were old letters? Something that could provide the answers she so desperately needed, especially now?

She had started back up the stairs, her legs still weak,

her heart still racing from their lovemaking, but the sound of the rainmaker's hammer clanging against the pipes reverberated inside her skull and sent her rushing from the house. That and the memory of the rainmaker's face.

Dulcie brushed the thought away as she waited for the schoolteacher. Jolene had been investigating Laura Beaumont's murder and apparently didn't want anyone to know. Dulcie couldn't wait to ask the schoolteacher why.

Jolene came out of the school and double-checked the door to make sure it was locked. Dulcie thought of how she'd done the same thing at the farmhouse. Was Jolene worried that someone had been getting in—just as Dulcie was? What else did they have in common? she wondered, as she followed the teacher to her house.

"I have some iced tea," Jolene said as she parked her bike against the side of the house and opened the front door.

"I'd love some."

Fans whirred in the windows, circulating the hot air. "Sorry, I don't have air-conditioning. Just have a seat anywhere," Jolene called from the kitchen.

Dulcie remained standing until Jolene returned. She took the tall, sweating glass offered her and sipped the tea. "This is wonderful. Thank you."

Jolene nodded, looking nervous. "I really don't know anything—"

"Let's sit down," Dulcie said, taking a seat across from her. "Why are you researching Laura Beaumont's death?"

"I was just curious."

"Why would you be interested in her murder? I know you aren't from around here. All I can assume is that you learned something about her death that made you curious."

"If you inherited the house then you know more about—"

"I never heard of Laura Beaumont until after my parents died and I was told I'd inherited property in Montana," Dulcie said. "I didn't even know there was a house on the land, let alone that the woman who'd left it to me had been murdered—or that she'd had a little girl."

Jolene took a sip of her tea.

Dulcie saw that her hands were trembling. "Jolene, some very strange things have been happening from the first time I laid eyes on that house. If you know something, please, help me."

"What kind of strange things?"

Dulcie sat back, holding the glass in both hands as if she could soak up the cold. She started at the beginning, telling about her elderly parents, her mother's trouble conceiving, the complete shock of the Montana property, her fear that she was Angel Beaumont.

"When I saw those yellow curtains…" She shook her head. "I know it sounds crazy, but I knew I'd seen them before. That wasn't all. There's a sound out there on the place…" Her voice broke.

"You felt you'd been there before?"

"I *know* I have. How else can I explain these feelings of déjà vu? I need to find the connection. Why leave this property to *me?*"

Jolene put down her glass. "You can't be Angel Beaumont. They found her drowned in the creek. She's buried up on the hill. I had planned to go up there—"

"What if she didn't drown in the creek? Come on, have you seen how shallow the creek is right now and this spring is just like that one. There wasn't enough water in the creek for her to drown."

Dulcie sighed. "I guess I want to believe she is

alive because it would explain why I inherited the property."

"But that would mean…"

She nodded. "That I'm Angel Beaumont. My parents had to have had a reason for keeping the Montana property a secret. I feel as if it was something they couldn't bring themselves to talk about. Something they had to let me discover on my own. I know that sounds strange."

"Not really."

"It's like they were…ashamed to talk about it. See? Crazy."

"Maybe not so crazy."

Dulcie studied the young woman over the rim of her glass. Jolene knew more than she was saying. If there was one thing Dulcie had learned in business, it was to be patient. Let the other person fill the silence.

"You're going to think *I'm* crazy now," Jolene said finally and gave a nervous laugh.

"Try me," Dulcie said.

"I get the feeling that the community knows something about the murder but they've made a secret pact not to tell."

"A conspiracy?" That didn't sound crazy to Dulcie at all.

Jolene nodded. "What if the little girl discovered her mother's body and she saw the killer? Since the killer was never caught and for all we know he still lives here, what if the community is protecting him?"

"Or protecting Angel Beaumont," Dulcie said. "Isn't it possible the community faked her death so the killer wouldn't find out she was alive?"

Jolene shivered and put down her glass. "The killer could be a woman."

Dulcie stared at her. "Why would you say that?"

"It's a possibility, isn't it?" Jolene picked up her tea again, avoiding Dulcie's gaze.

She'd been right. Jolene knew something. That's why she'd researched the murder at the newspaper office.

"You never told me what got you interested in this murder case," Dulcie said.

Jolene slowly raised her gaze to meet hers. "How do I know I can trust you?"

"Because I can tell you're terrified for some reason," Dulcie said. "So am I."

Jolene studied her openly for a moment, then rose and went to the drawer in a cabinet. She took out some papers and, holding them against her chest, returned to her chair and sat down.

"I gave my students a short-story assignment. The story is to continue for six days with a small part turned in each day until the story ends on the last day."

She glanced down at the papers she held tightly against her chest. "The first day I got an extra story. Someone had left it on an empty desk in the school-house. The story is about the murder of a widow who had a young daughter."

Dulcie wasn't sure what she'd expected but definitely not this. "Laura Beaumont?"

"That would be my guess."

"Who is leaving you the story?"

"I have no idea. Apparently, some of the residents have keys to the school, so it could be anyone."

"This story, do you have reason to believe it's not fictional?"

"It takes place during a hot spring just like this one. It reads as if it was written by someone who knew the murder victim, someone who watched her and her daughter."

Dulcie felt her heart begin to race faster. "Someone who might know who killed her?"

"Possibly."

Her gaze went to the pages Jolene held. She was trying to be patient. "Why would this person give it to you, do you think?"

"At first I thought they just wanted me to read their story and critique it."

"And now?"

"Now I'm afraid it might be a confession."

Dulcie sat forward. "May I read it?"

Jolene seemed to hesitate for a second before she handed it over. "It's only the first four days' worth. There are still two more segments. One tomorrow, with the ending on Monday. At least I hope there is an ending."

"We already know how it ends," Dulcie said absently, her attention on the papers in her hands.

"Do we?" Jolene said. "I'm not so sure about that."

Chapter Nine

Russell spent the remainder of the afternoon making sure Finnegan Amherst didn't return to Dulcie's farmhouse.

Watching the rainmaker work only convinced him that he and the other ranchers and farmers had just thrown away fifteen thousand dollars.

"So where did you learn this?" he'd asked Finnegan.

"I met an old Indian who could make rain. He taught me everything he knew."

Finnegan had driven a series of steel pipes into the ground near the water along the creek. Occasionally he would stop, listen for a long while, then uproot a pipe and sink it elsewhere.

"And the purpose of the steel pipes?"

"They act as an antenna to redirect the energy flow." He must have heard the skepticism in Russell's voice. "I don't *make* rain, Mr. Corbett. Only God makes it rain. I *influence* the weather. The earth is your mother." He lifted his arms and raised his face toward the heavens. "I reach out to her to redirect the jet stream." As he dropped his hands, he added, "Prayer is good, too."

"Have you ever *not* made it rain?" Russell had to ask.

The rainmaker smiled his twisted smile, the dark

eyes shining. "Ranchers have been known to string up men who don't make it rain. I'm still alive, aren't I?"

When Finnegan finally quit for the day to return to his tent at Trafton Park in Whitehorse, Russell had gone by the farmhouse to check on Dulcie.

Seeing that she'd gone left him torn between disappointment and worry. What would she do next? Maybe she'd given up on this quest to find out more about Laura Beaumont and had returned to Chicago. Without saying goodbye?

That thought filled him with a sense of loss for a woman he'd known less than forty-eight hours. But then again, a woman like Dulcie Hughes got under a man's skin immediately.

He told himself she wouldn't leave without telling him goodbye, but he wasn't completely sure about that. He was, however, sure she wasn't the kind to give up easily and he doubted she'd solved the mystery this afternoon in that old house.

As he drove toward the ranch, he thought he must have conjured her from his imagination because a car like Dulcie's rental was headed down the road toward him right now, coming from the wrong direction.

Why would she be coming from Old Town Whitehorse?

He slowed the pickup, pulling to the side to let her pass.

She slowed and then seemed to reluctantly pull to a stop next to his pickup. He waited as she whirred down her window and smiled but not before he'd seen the exhaustion in her face.

"You look tired," he said.

She didn't deny it, confirming that she was dead on her feet. The strain of her quest, no doubt.

"Have you had anything to eat?"

"Breakfast," she said with the quirk of her mouth. "It gave me indigestion."

"I don't think it was the food. Park your rig in that turnoff behind you and come with me. No arguments for once in your life."

She smiled at that and surprisingly didn't put up a fight, instead backing her car into the turnoff to a pasture. He pulled up, reached over to open the passenger's-side door and she climbed in. As he drove toward the ranch, she leaned back in the seat and closed her eyes.

"Where are you taking me?" she asked, sounding as if it really didn't make any difference.

"You'll see. How was your day?"

"Fine." She opened her eyes and looked over at him. "I don't want to talk about it, okay?"

He glanced at her, saw her expression and said, "Okay."

She closed her eyes again and they drove in a companionable silence until he slowed for the turnoff to the ranch.

She sat up. "Trails West Ranch?" Glancing over at him, she asked, "Are you sure this is a good idea?"

It was a terrible idea for a lot of reasons, he thought. "I thought you'd like to meet my family."

"If this is about buying my property—"

"This is about getting you a good meal," he said. "Nothing more."

She cut her eyes to him as he parked in front of the main house.

"I hope you like margaritas," he said as he got out and led her toward the front door.

DULCIE STEPPED INTO THE cool, inviting ranch house and was drawn to the voices and muffled laughter. She breathed in the smell of tantalizing Mexican food cooking somewhere close by and could almost taste the sharp, tangy salt on the rim of a margarita as Russell took her arm and called out, "I brought a friend for supper."

The night passed in a pleasant blur of good food, drink and company. The Corbetts were a handsome and charming bunch and she liked their stepmother, Kate, a lot. She complimented Juanita on her amazing culinary masterpieces and thanked Kate and Grayson for allowing her to join them.

"You should have warned me," Dulcie said on the way back to her car after the evening was over.

"Would you have gone with me if I had warned you about my family?"

"You know I didn't mean your family," she said, humor in her voice. "You're one of those wealthy ranchers I've heard about."

"I work."

"I know you do," she said, taking his right hand from the wheel and running her fingertips along the callouses. "That's one of the things I like about you."

"*One* of the things?"

"You? Fishing for compliments?" she said, shoving his hand away with a laugh. "I wasn't exactly honest with you either about my work." She told him about Renada and the boutique they started that grew into a wildly successful enterprise.

"What will you do now?" he asked.

"I don't know. Not sit idle, that's not me. But truthfully, I'm out of ideas at the moment. This thing with the property and that house…"

"I visited this morning with someone who used to own the property behind yours by the creek."

"Where your rainmaker is working."

His rainmaker. He grimaced inwardly. "John and Midge Atkinson. They moved into town after the murder, I think. I was hoping to get some answers for you, but…"

"But people don't want to talk about it, do they?"

"No."

"Doesn't that tell you something?" she asked, glancing over at him, her face intent in the glow of the dashboard lights.

"What it tells me is that people don't like talking about the brutal murder of a young woman who lived near them, someone they knew. I get the impression that Midge Atkinson was a friend of hers."

Dulcie started. "Midge Atkinson? No wonder the name sounded familiar. An M. Atkinson painted angels on the wall in Angel Beaumont's bedroom upstairs. Do you know if Midge paints?"

"Could be. All the borders were painted at her house. But if she was a friend, then that could explain why some people don't want to talk about the murder."

"Maybe they don't want to talk because the killer was never caught…and he's someone in this community and they're all covering for him."

Russell shot her a look. "Is that what you think?"

"I'M NOT THE ONLY ONE who thinks that." Dulcie regretted the words instantly.

"Someone told you *that*?" He slowed as her car came into view.

"I'm sorry I said it."

"But not because it wasn't true." He stopped the pickup and looked over at her. "Dulcie, you're scaring me. If you know something, you have to go to the sheriff. Or talk to my brother Shane. You met him tonight. He's a deputy sheriff. He'll help you." Shane had left just before them for his late shift.

"I don't know *anything,* that's the problem. It's all speculation."

He studied her openly in the dashboard light. "You aren't going to let this go, are you? Then let me help you. I don't want you to have to do this alone."

"Thank you. For the offer. For supper. For including me in your family tonight."

"I'm serious about helping you," he said.

It was tempting to accept his help. But what could he do? The locals weren't apt to talk to him any more than they were to her. Russell hadn't been here long enough that he knew the community's secrets. Maybe you had to go back five generations for that.

"I know you are serious about helping me and I appreciate that. I just don't know how you can help me right now."

"You're going back to the house tomorrow."

She nodded. It was all she had.

"Then let me come with you. I'll scare away the snakes and do whatever you need."

"And make sure your rainmaker doesn't come back?"

"That, too."

She shook her head. Tomorrow she planned to cross the creek and talk to the rainmaker. After reading the murder story Jolene had given her, Dulcie had some leverage to use with him. The only way she might get the rainmaker to talk to her, though, was if Russell Corbett was nowhere around.

"If I need you, I'll let you know." She opened the passenger's-side door. "I liked your family."

"Well, that was only because they were on their best behavior tonight."

"Oh?" She hadn't meant to sound so suspicious.

"My father and I are the only ones who discussed purchasing your land—if and when you put it up for sale."

"So why were they on their best behavior?" she asked.

"It's embarrassing."

"They thought I was your girlfriend?" She laughed. "They must be horrified. You and a fool city girl? I heard what you muttered under your breath the first day we met."

He leaned back, smiling over at her. "Now I *am* embarrassed."

"No, you're not. Anyway, it's true. I *am* a fool city girl out here and gone in the wilds of Montana." She glanced away for a moment. "I don't even know what I'm doing here."

"Looking for answers."

"That's what I keep telling myself. But I'm not sure I want to hear the answers."

"Then why keep looking? You can walk away right now."

She laughed at how outrageous that was.

"I'm serious."

"I know you are, but nothing could get me to quit at this point. I have the feeling that the reason my parents didn't tell me about this property was because this was something I had to do myself and they knew it."

He shook his head. "This is no way to find it out about a murdered woman and her dead child." He sounded angry.

"You didn't know my parents."

"Did *you?*" he shot back.

She started to step out of the pickup.

"I'm sorry, you're right, I didn't know your parents. I should keep my opinions to myself."

She couldn't be angry with him. Russell had been there for her when she'd needed him and she hadn't forgotten when they'd made love in the house.

But he couldn't solve this for her—as much as he wanted to. "Thank you again for this evening. I can't tell you how much I needed it but then I think you knew that, didn't you?"

"You give me too much credit."

"No, I don't." She thought about leaning back into the pickup's cab and kissing him. But she knew how dangerous that would be. The two of them being intimate again wasn't a good idea.

Instead, she smiled, stepped out of the truck and closed the door.

He waited, just as she'd known he would, for her to start her car and drive down the road before he turned around and headed back to the ranch.

She didn't let herself think about the copy of the murder story Jolene Stevens had given her until his pickup's taillights disappeared from her rearview mirror. Shuddering, she glanced over at the story stuffed in her shoulder bag.

Was it just fiction? Or was Jolene Stevens right? Could it be a confession? But why write it for the teacher of the one-room schoolhouse?

And where, if anywhere, did that leave Dulcie?

The headlights came out of nowhere. One minute there was no one behind her. The next a pickup was tailgating her, its bright lights blinding.

Dulcie slowed a little, pulling to the side to let the impatient driver pass.

The pickup started past her, then swerved into her rental. The loud crunch of metal filled the car as she was thrown against the door. Her car veered to the right. She fought to keep it on the road as it swerved wildly.

At first she thought the truck had hit her accidentally until the driver swerved into her again, jarring her vehicle in a roar of engine and screaming metal.

Ahead the road narrowed, dropping off steeply on both sides. The truck swerved away from her after the impact, but she could see it heading for her again.

She sped up, knowing her only chance was to outrun the driver.

The pickup fell in behind her, the lights filling the cab as it stayed with her. The road dipped and rose. The car caught air over a rise and came down hard.

Behind her, the truck came off the top of the rise airborne. It was going so fast that for a breathtaking instant, she thought it would land on her.

The pickup came down in a cloud of dust directly behind her. She felt it slam into the back of her car, shooting her forward before the truck started to fishtail in some loose gravel on the edge of the recently graded road.

In her side mirror she saw the truck leave the road, barreling down into the barrow pit and back up the other side. It hurtled through a barbed-wire fence before coming to rest in a mushroom cloud of dust in the middle of a wheat field.

Dulcie sped up, racing toward town. In her rearview mirror she saw the truck's headlights sweep around as the driver headed back toward the road.

Fear had her gripping the wheel and continuing to glance at the rearview mirror. She was driving as fast as she could without going off the road herself, afraid any moment the pickup's headlights would appear again over a rise.

But a few turns in the road, she looked back and saw nothing but darkness behind her. Either the pickup hadn't been able to get out of the wheat field, or whoever had tried to run her off the road had given up, having successfully sent their message.

She didn't slow until she reached the outskirts of town. Her heart was still pounding as she drove down the main drag looking for the sheriff's department.

The office was in a small brick building. She was glad to see Shane Corbett as she rushed in.

"What's wrong?" he asked as he saw her face.

"Someone just tried to run me off the road." She motioned toward her rental car parked outside.

"Let me have a look. Stay here." And he was gone. A few minutes later he returned. "Come into the office and I'll take your report."

By then she wasn't shaking anymore and was able to tell him what she could about the truck. "Dark colored." She saw by his expression that the description wasn't going to help. "There are a lot of dark-colored trucks around here, aren't there?"

He nodded. "But the driver left some paint on your rental car. The pickup was brown and I would imagine you left some bright red paint on his pickup. We'll look for it and have the body shop watch for it."

She doubted the truck would be turning up. The driver would be a fool not to park it in his barn and leave it there.

"Any reason someone would want to run you off the road?"

"No." Even as she said it, she wondered if she was wrong.

"Did the driver appear to be drunk?"

"Not really."

"I guess what I'm asking is if you were going too slow and taking up the road?" he said, looking embarrassed.

"You mean being a city girl?" She sighed. "No, I was going normal speed and I even pulled over to let him go around and he wouldn't."

Shane nodded. "Didn't mean to insult you. Just trying to figure out why anyone would want to run you off the road."

"I haven't been here long enough to make enemies, but I have been looking into Laura Beaumont's murder."

He nodded slowly. "Russell mentioned that. You know—"

"You aren't going to tell me that I might be putting myself in danger by doing that, are you?"

Shane smiled. Those Corbett men really were good-looking. "I might have thought about warning you that sometimes locals don't take kindly to a newcomer butting into their business."

"That's what I thought. But isn't it more likely that, since the murder was never solved, I'm making someone nervous?"

"A twenty-four-year-old murder? The killer's gone free all this time? Seems kind of stupid for him to try to run you off the road and give himself away when you don't have any evidence against him, right?"

He did have a point.

"Not yet," she admitted.

"Yeah, that's the part that makes me nervous," he said. "What exactly are you thinking of doing to find this evidence?"

"Just doing a little more digging."

He raised an eyebrow. "You think that's a good idea?"

"Someone is trying to scare me off. That means there is something to find and I don't scare off easily."

"I'm beginning to see why my brother is so taken with you—and why he's equally as worried."

"He's *taken* with me?" she asked with a grin.

"You tell him I said that and I'll deny it. Seriously, we're a small sheriff's department. There's no way we can protect you."

"But you could *help* me," Dulcie said. "You could let me see the file on Laura Beaumont's murder."

She ran blind from her mother's bedroom, leaving bloody footprints. The killer raced after her, calling her name, as she ran down the stairs and burst out the front door.

She could hear the killer behind her as they both disappeared into the darkness. It wasn't until she reached the road that she realized she'd run the wrong way.

Had she run toward the creek, she could have hidden in the trees. Or called her friend for help. He would've saved her.

But instead she'd run to the road.

She looked back, hearing the killer coming behind her, knowing now that she didn't stand a chance of getting away. The killer was almost to the open gate. On the road the killer would have no trouble catching her.

Lights came over the small hill, blinding her. She closed her eyes at the screech of brakes and thrown gravel as the vehicle skidded to a stop. She was caught in the headlights like a deer about to be slaughtered.

The door opened. "Angel? My God, Angel, is that

*blood on you? Where's your mama? Tell me where your
mama is, girl. Stop your crying and pulling away, I'm
not hurting you. Tell me what's happened. Stop it and
tell me what your mama has done now."*

*It rained the day of Angel Beaumont's funeral. She
was buried on the hill overlooking Old Town Whitehorse. The whole county turned out, huddled under a
sea of black umbrellas, as Titus Cavanaugh read from
the Bible and prayed over the poor helpless child.*

*During the funeral the rainmaker drove by in his
beat-up truck, his magical pipes singing against each
other. The mourners dispersed soon after. A few days
later, the community had joined again at the cemetery
to lay to rest the mother now beside the child, just as
they had laid to rest the truth.*

JOLENE LOOKED UP AT HER Friday class, heart pounding. All but one head was bent over the math assignment
she'd handed out. Her unruly fifth-grader, Thad Brooks,
was chewing on the end of his pencil and staring out the
window, daydreaming.

She cleared her throat, catching his attention. He
ducked his head and went back to work. She read the
pages again.

Last night she'd tossed and turned for hours, afraid
she'd made a mistake by giving Dulcie copies of the
murder story. She'd been anxious this morning to get
the next assignment, equally afraid the author would
find out what she'd done and quit sending it.

Now she'd been given another piece of the puzzle and
she couldn't wait to see what Dulcie thought about it.

When her students had finished their math assignment and turned it in, Jolene said, "Monday is the last
day of your writing project, which means you have to

wind up your story. Today we're going to talk about endings. Can someone tell me what we need to do to make a satisfying ending?"

"What if we can't end it?" Mace Carpenter asked. "Cuz it has no ending?"

"For this assignment, you need to end it," she said. "The ending of your story must satisfy all the questions the person reading your story might have. For instance, the reader will want to know what happened to your character. Why it happened. And feel satisfied that the character will be all right in the future."

"That's called a happy ending," Codi spoke up. "Which means your character can't die, isn't that right, Miss Stevens?"

"For this assignment I think it best if your characters continue living, yes." She wasn't sure why she'd just told them that the stories had to have a happy ending. They didn't. Maybe because she hoped there would be a happy ending to the mystery in the murder story.

At recess, Jolene made a decision. She called the cell phone number Dulcie had given her, planning to leave a message. She was surprised when Dulcie answered and said as much.

"I'm in town. I had to wait until my new rental car was delivered. It's a long story. Did you get another part of the murder story?" she asked excitedly.

"Yes." She glanced around to make sure no one was nearby listening and then read the story.

"The girl is alive," Dulcie cried.

"Not necessarily. The person who found her certainly wasn't very compassionate."

"What are you saying? That you think the person in the vehicle killed her? That the killer had an accomplice?"

"Maybe. I don't know. I guess it depends on who

found her that night and why that person wasn't very kind to her, if you believe the author of the story."

Dulcie was quiet for a moment. "I still think she's alive, but you're right. It doesn't mention what happens to the killer. I wonder what the author of the story is trying to tell us."

Tell *us?* Jolene shuddered. The author was trying to tell *her* something, but Jolene wasn't sure what exactly.

"If Angel lived, then that would explain why no one wants to talk about what happened to the girl. She saw the killer. She could identify him."

"So why didn't she identify him?" Jolene asked in a whisper.

This time Dulcie was silent for much longer. "I hadn't thought of that. She was old enough to identify the killer. Unless she didn't recognize him. Still, she could have described him. Unless she was too traumatized to do so."

Jolene knew where Dulcie was headed with this. "So you think the community secreted her away so the killer couldn't find her."

"Or so she *couldn't* identify the killer."

Jolene shuddered at the thought.

"They found someone to adopt her. Apparently Laura didn't have any family. It makes sense. Especially if I'm Angel Beaumont."

It *did* make sense, Jolene thought. And that's what was scaring her.

THE MOMENT RUSSELL saw his brother drive up, he knew something had happened and he feared it had to do with Dulcie Hughes.

"I'll be back in a minute," he told the ranch hands

he'd been working with on the new section of fence and hurried toward the patrol car as Shane got out.

Russell had been out since sunup, hoping to work off some of his frustration. He would have liked to forget all about Dulcie Hughes, but there didn't seem much chance of that. Now he was convinced he'd had every right to be worried.

"What's she done now?" he asked before his brother had a chance to open his mouth.

"She got into a little fender bender on the way home last night," Shane said, knowing at once who he was referring to. He quickly added, "She wasn't hurt."

"A fender bender?"

"A pickup tried to run her off the road."

Russell swore as his mind raced to make sense of it. "Why would someone…" His voice trailed off as he realized his brother hadn't driven all this way out here to tell him that.

"We found a pickup that matches the description she gave us. It has some of her fancy rental-car paint on the side of it," Shane said.

"*Who?* Did you arrest the son-of-a-bitch?"

Shane held up a hand. "It's a little more complicated than that. The pickup is a beater John Atkinson keeps down in his barn on his old ranch."

"Let me guess, he told you he keeps the key in the ignition?" Russell demanded sarcastically.

"On the floorboard. He swears he hasn't used the truck in months and didn't know it was missing until this morning when he happened down that way and found it in the ditch with a flat tire."

"And you believe him?"

"I do. The pickup reeked of alcohol. If John had tried to run someone off the road in it, seems kind of dumb of him to just leave it in a ditch right beside the road since it didn't take five minutes to trace the truck back to him."

Russell swore. "You're telling me you think some drunk kids borrowed the truck for a joy ride?"

"Looks that way."

"Bet Dulcie didn't see it that way," Russell said, narrowing his eyes at his brother.

Shane sighed. "Nope. She thinks someone is trying to scare her off this investigation she's doing of Laura Beaumont's murder. She even asked to see the file."

"Did you let her?"

"You know better than that on an unsolved case." He shook his head. "I did go dig the file out of cold-case storage. Brutal murder. The woman was stabbed thirteen times."

"A crime of passion?"

"She did have some men friends, apparently."

"John Atkinson?" Russell saw that his brother wanted to deny it, but couldn't.

"He *was* questioned. He had an alibi for the time of the murder. He was with his wife."

"Midge." Russell thought about his visit to the Atkinsons. Now their reactions made a hell of a lot more sense. "Did you ever think that Dulcie might know what she's talking about? That the killer is still around?"

"I'm not arguing that. I just don't believe that's what was going on last night, given the evidence."

Russell wanted to argue further, but he could see it would be a waste of breath. That and the fact that Shane Corbett was a damned good law-enforcement officer who'd been a Texas Ranger and was now a local deputy with a hell of a lot of experience.

Not that even the best weren't taken in on occasion by a clever criminal. But this criminal didn't sound clever.

Laura's killer sounded like someone who'd lost control. Or maybe never had much control.

"Just tell me this," he said to his brother. "Was Ben Carpenter one of the other men who were questioned during the murder investigation?"

Shane seemed surprised. "No, should he have been?"

"Maybe." Russell saw that his brother was chewing on his cheek and realized there was more, something Shane was debating whether or not to tell him.

"What else did you find in the file? I know there's more."

Shane looked away for a moment. "The file had been sealed by a local judge."

"Sealed?" Russell asked in surprise. "In an unsolved murder case? I thought they only did that when a juvenile was involved?"

"I guess they did it because of the little girl."

"Angel Beaumont. But she's dead."

Shane said nothing.

"She is dead, right?"

"Her death certificate was signed by the same judge."

Russell swore.

"Now, don't go jumping to conclusions," Shane warned. "The judge was probably acting as coroner back then."

"Don't give me that. You think something is wrong with this case or you wouldn't have just told me about this."

Shane cocked his head at him. "How involved are you with this woman?" He swore as he caught Russell's expression. "Hell, Russell."

"It isn't like I'm falling for her." Russell couldn't

regret making love with Dulcie, no matter how big a fool move it had been. "She'll be gone back to Chicago soon."

Shane was shaking his head and frowning. "Look," he said. "I found something in the file. I'm sure Dulcie is going to find out about it sooner or later. Maybe sooner and from someone who cares about her would be better."

Russell held his breath.

"Laura Beaumont's maiden name was Hughes. She was the daughter of Brad and Kathy Hughes of Chicago—and the mother of *two* daughters. Angel was the *oldest*."

Chapter Ten

After making plans to meet Jolene later, Dulcie called Renada. She felt terrible for not doing it sooner.

"Honey, you sound awful. Put the property up for sale and get out of there," Renada said.

"It's not that simple." She had skipped telling her friend about Laura's murder or about Angel Beaumont. "I still don't know why it was left to me and until I do, I can't leave."

"How did I know you were going to say that? Have you at least met a handsome cowboy?"

"Actually…"

Renada laughed. "I can't wait to hear all about it. You're sure you don't need me to come out there?"

"Positive. How is the design class going?"

"Wonderful! I am having so much fun. I'll tell you all about it when you get back. Back soon, okay?"

"Okay." Dulcie hung up and felt like crying. She missed her friend, but she knew it was more than that. She was scared. She'd been scared ever since she'd heard she'd inherited the property in Montana.

And it had only gotten worse once she'd arrived here and found out what had happened to Laura Beaumont and her daughter.

She was convinced she was Angel Beaumont. It was

the only thing that made any sense, she told herself, as she drove to the farmhouse. And if there was one person who might tell her the truth it was the rainmaker.

She'd seen his shocked expression yesterday on the stairs. For a moment she would swear he'd thought she was Laura Beaumont. Was it possible she resembled the woman?

According to the short story, the rainmaker had known Laura intimately. He would have seen the little girl.

Dulcie followed the banging of his hammer, heard it slow as she approached, and then cease. The rainmaker raised his head as if he'd sensed her more than had seen her coming.

With one filthy hand, he pushed back his hat and leveled those malevolent dark eyes at her.

"What do you want?" he asked, his sandpaper voice grating.

"You knew Laura Beaumont."

His expression didn't change.

"I know you were her lover."

One eyebrow lifted, but he still said nothing.

"I need to know about her and her daughter."

He chuckled at that, a dry, rusty sound. "You need to mind your own business."

"It *is* my business. If you know who killed her—"

"If I knew, he'd be dead." The words snapped like a whip.

Dulcie swallowed, not doubting for an instant that he meant it. "I saw your expression yesterday when you glanced up as I came down the stairs. Do I look like Laura?"

"I have work to do." He reached for his sledgehammer.

She grabbed his arm. It was hard and strong as the

steel he pounded. "Please, I have to know why you thought I was Laura Beaumont."

"You're not." He jerked his arm free.

"I could be her daughter, Angel."

The dark eyes narrowed. "You're not."

"How do you know that?"

A thin, cold smile curled his lips. "I'm sure. Go home before you get hurt."

"Are you threatening me?" Her voice betrayed her and broke, making him smile as he picked up the sledge-hammer.

"Leave me alone." He turned his back on her. As he swung the hammer, she had to jump back. He brought the sledge down hard on the top of the steel pipe. The deafening sound rang in her ears long after she left.

RUSSELL HAD RIDDEN OUT this morning to help with the fence. Now he realized that he could get to the old Beaumont place faster by horseback than returning to the ranch for his pickup.

He needed the fresh air anyway. The news his brother had given him only made him more afraid for Dulcie.

That Dulcie had been right about a possible cover-up only made him more anxious. Now there definitely seemed to be a question as to whether or not Angel Beaumont was really dead. If Angel had seen the killer, that would explain why her mother's murder file had been sealed. Someone had wanted the townspeople to believe that Angel was dead.

But was she?

It was all speculation with few facts and he knew better than to jump to too many conclusions at this point.

Or had sealing the file been about protecting the second daughter so she didn't end up like Angel?

As he rode past part of the Atkinson place, he saw John standing out by his barn and on impulse rode over. John shielded his eyes and, seeing him, let out a curse.

"Let's see this old truck my brother told me about," Russell said as he dismounted.

"What are you doing, getting involved in this?" John demanded. "It doesn't have anything to do with you."

"Seems to have something to do with Dulcie Hughes, though, doesn't it?"

John shook his head irritably. "I told your brother—"

"I know what you told my brother and I know what you told me yesterday. How about telling me the truth?"

"Damn it, I didn't have anything to do with that woman being run off the road last night."

"But you did have something to do with Laura Beaumont."

"I suppose your brother the deputy already told you I had an affair with Laura."

"Actually, I figured that out on my own."

"Midge knows all about it."

"Is that why she gave you an alibi the day of the murder?"

John looked angry again. "I didn't kill Laura. I loved her. I was planning to leave Midge for her if—"

"If what?"

"If she hadn't dumped me for someone else, all right?"

"Who?"

John looked away, his jaw set, and for a moment Russell thought he wouldn't answer. "Ben Carpenter. At least that's who I saw going into her house right after I left."

"You must have been angry enough to kill her."

John swore and started to walk away, but turned back. "I *loved* her. I wouldn't have hurt her for…" He wagged his head, looking miserable. "I would have done *anything* for her."

"What about Midge?"

"What about her?"

"If she found out about you and Laura, maybe—"

"She'd known for months. She was the one who told me there were other men. I didn't believe her until I saw it for myself."

"And you did *nothing?*"

John let out a humorless laugh. "Wrong. I did something. I crawled back to my wife and begged her forgiveness."

"Is that when you moved to the other ranch?"

John nodded, looking shamefaced. "And before you bother to ask, I was cleaning out one of the bedrooms to move our stuff in when I heard about Laura. It damn near killed me. I've never gotten over Laura. I never will."

"So tell me what you know about Laura and her two daughters."

DULCIE HAD SEARCHED the house for hours. She had just stepped out for a breath of fresh air when she saw the lone rider coming over the hill across the road.

She'd wondered if Russell's brother would tell him about the pickup that had tried to run her off the road. It had surprised her she hadn't heard from Russ. She'd expected him to come tearing up, angry and scared and dispensing more good advice.

One look at the expression on his handsome face now, though, and she knew he must have only just heard about last night.

She leaned against the side of the house in the shade

and watched as he rode the large buckskin horse into her yard. He swung off the horse like a man as at home in a saddle as on a four-wheeler or driving a combine.

She hadn't been able to help the small thrill she had felt seeing him astride the horse. Riding to her rescue, she thought with a grin.

"Something amusing?" he asked as he walked to the bottom of the porch steps.

"Just admiring you in the saddle."

He climbed the steps in long strides that brought him right to her. She could tell by the look on his face that he wasn't here to make love to her again.

"My brother tell you that he found the pickup that ran you off the road?" he asked. "He thinks some kids took it from an old barn, picked up some booze and went for a joy ride."

Her brown eyes narrowed. "What do *you* think?"

"I think anyone who knows John knows about that pickup. They probably saw your car parked where we left it yesterday evening and just waited at a distance for you to return."

"So you think it was a warning, too?"

He shook his head. "A warning would have been a note tacked on your door."

She thought about the note Jolene told her had been tucked under her windshield wiper. *Watch your step.*

She nodded, her gaze locked with his.

He dragged his away. "You look good."

"I'll just bet after being in that house all day, digging into every dirty corner I could find."

"I take it you didn't find anything?"

She shook her head.

Russell glanced toward the house behind her. "You searched the whole place?"

She nodded.

"Then maybe it's time for you to go back to Chicago."

That took her by surprise. "Just when we're having so much fun?" she said, trying to make light of it.

"I stopped having fun when someone tried to hurt you," he said quietly, his incredible blue eyes locking with hers.

Dulcie swallowed the lump in her throat as she saw that he was no longer teasing. He was dead serious and she felt the intensity of his gaze all the way down to her toes.

"There is something I need to tell you," he said and she felt her heart drop. "You've been trying to find out about Laura Beaumont's past…"

She saw it in his face. He was about to deliver some devastating news.

"Laura's maiden name was Hughes. She was the daughter of Brad and Kathy Hughes of Chicago. She had two daughters."

Dulcie grabbed the porch railing as the world tilted crazily and suddenly she could no longer get enough oxygen into her lungs.

RUSSELL STEPPED UP BEHIND her and wrapped his arms around her. He could feel her shock, her pain, her disbelief in the rigid muscles of her body.

He'd feared what this would do to her, finding out that the murdered woman who'd lived in this house had been her mother and that the little girl who had died was her sister.

Dulcie was strong, stronger than any woman he'd ever met, but was she strong enough to get past this?

Her words came out a whisper. "The oldest daughter? What was her name?"

"Angel Lee."

"And the youngest?"

He swallowed. "Dulcie Ann."

"I don't understand."

"John Atkinson told me that Laura had gotten in a lot of trouble when she was young. She'd run away and married Darrell Beaumont against your grandparents' wishes. They disowned her."

He felt Dulcie stiffen, waited a moment, and continued. "Laura had two children right away, one right after the other. When Darrell was killed in a motorcycle accident, Laura contacted your parents for help. She was living here in the old Beaumont place, Darrell's family was helping out, but Laura was lonely and lost. Are you sure you want to hear this?"

She nodded, but didn't turn around.

"Your grandparents came to Whitehorse. Laura apparently thought they'd come to take her back to Chicago but when she realized it would be on their terms, she turned them down. They saw the way she was living here and insisted on taking you back with them since you were the youngest, only three at the time. They apparently raised you as their own."

Dulcie shook her head and stepped out of his arms to go to the end of the porch. "I can't believe they would do that."

"This is only Laura's side of the story through someone else. Angel refused to go with them. She said she had to stay and take care of her mother." He knew she deserved to be angry, but said, "I'm sure your grandparents didn't know how to tell you after everything that happened."

She turned. Her face was still pale, but her eyes were fired with heat. "Yes, how could they explain what they'd done? Taking me, leaving behind my sister to..." She waved an arm through the air. "And then not telling me all those years, letting me walk into this minefield?"

"Parents make mistakes."

"Don't even try to defend them."

He stood listening to the pounding of his heart and realized he could no longer hear Finnegan Amherst sinking the metal pipes. Glancing at the sky, he saw nothing but blue sky. Not a cloud in sight. "Dulcie—"

"It makes sense now, doesn't it?" she said with a bitter laugh. "Me inheriting the property. I knew there had to be a connection, but I never dreamed..."

"I'm sorry you had to find out this way. John told me that Laura wore a locket around her neck with your picture in it. She would never take it off. He said losing you broke her heart."

Dulcie's eyes welled with tears. She quickly turned away.

He started to go to her, but stopped himself, giving her the space he knew she needed. "John said Laura feared they would come back for Angel, as well. He thinks it was the reason she wanted to remarry, but only someone she could love as much as your father. I'm so sorry you had to find out this way."

"So they left Angel and then Laura was murdered and Angel..." She turned around. "What happened to Angel?"

"She died, Dulcie. You were the child everyone was trying to protect."

Dulcie shook her head. "That can't be right." She glanced at her watch. "I have to go."

"*Go?* Dulcie—"

"I'll be all right." She stepped to him to lay her palm against his cheek. "Thank you for telling me. I know how hard it was for you. I knew it was going to be something like this. I thought I must be Angel…" She shook her head and turned to go down the porch steps as if she had somewhere she had to get in a hurry.

Russell wanted to call her back, afraid for her.

She stopped at her car, looked back at him and smiled. "I want to ride a horse before I leave Montana. Promise?"

He nodded as she ducked into her car and stood watching her go, telling himself she needed time alone to digest all of this.

But as he watched her drive off, he knew that nothing would stop her from looking for the killer now.

DULCIE TOLD HERSELF THAT nothing had changed. She was still the same person she'd believed herself to be all these years. But she was lying—just as everyone had lied to her.

She didn't know who she was, wasn't sure she could get past this. Her entire life had been built on the facade of a solid foundation that had now crumbled to dust and she felt herself sinking into the mire of lies.

Her mind whirled as she drove. A mother and father she'd never known. Her parents…*grand*parents, the two people she trusted the most. She could see their faces, the worry in them from the time she could remember. So much older than all her classmates' parents.

"Why didn't you tell me the truth?" she cried, slamming her fist against the steering wheel. "Because you were cowards? Because…" The answer came to her as if plucked out of the blue sky overhead.

"Because you didn't want to tell me about my mother." She said the words on a ragged breath, her voice breaking as she thought of the murder story and the way Laura

Beaumont had been portrayed. An alley cat in heat. A mother who ignored her little girl.

But why hadn't her grandparents taken both girls? Why had they left Angel?

As she hit the brakes to make the curve in the road, Dulcie realized she was driving too fast. The car fishtailed wildly, the back tires sliding off into the shallow barrow pit. The sound of the dirt and gravel scraping across the underbelly of the rental car drowned out everything except the erratic pounding of her pulse. She was going to wreck another rental car. As if that was her biggest concern.

She got the car under control and slowed, her hands trembling on the wheel, her whole body shaking. The tears finally came in a rush, a wall of water that forced her to pull over and stop. She leaned on the steering wheel and cried for the mother and father and sister she'd never known, for the two people who had raised her, for herself.

When the sobs finally ceased, she wiped her eyes and pulled herself together. She might not know who she was—but she knew what she had to do. She straightened up and got the car going again, telling herself she'd always been strong. Now more than ever she needed that strength for what was coming.

She felt a small shiver of fear prickle her skin as she saw the Old Town Whitehorse cemetery ahead.

AFTER SCHOOL, JOLENE waited until everyone was gone before she walked up to the cemetery on the hill to meet Dulcie. The afternoon sun hung low in the sky after another torturous day of heat.

She stopped to catch her breath and pick some of the wildflowers that grew at the edge of the road. As she took her small bouquet and passed under the wrought-iron arch that read Whitehorse Cemetery to climb the hill, each breath burned her lungs.

The quiet up there was eerie. A stray gust of breeze stirred a bouquet of plastic flowers on a nearby grave. The air that brushed her face was hot as a fevered touch. She drew back instinctively and stood for a moment, trying to catch her breath.

She had to stop letting her imagination run away with her. There were no ghosts in this graveyard. The stories of the lights were nothing more than rural legends.

But the fear she felt was real as she saw Dulcie's rental car parked at the back of the cemetery. Was she waiting in her car? Or had she already found Angel Beaumont's grave?

Jolene wished she hadn't agreed to meet here. Normally she found cemeteries interesting. She liked the headstones, the history, the feeling of peace.

But today she felt jumpy.

Dulcie looked up as she approached. Something in her face made Jolene's heart lodge in her throat. Dulcie had discovered something. What?

All her fears came in a rush, filling her with terror. Perspiration beaded on her upper lip. She wiped at it and forced herself to walk over to where Dulcie waited.

She sucked in an arid breath, tears suddenly burning her eyes as Dulcie stepped to her.

"Why are you looking at me like that?" Jolene demanded, her voice a hoarse whisper. "What's happened?"

Dulcie shook her head and Jolene saw her hurriedly brush at her own tears. "I need to ask you something. How did you get the teaching position here?"

Suddenly she felt dizzy, a little confused. She shook

her head as if to clear it. "Someone called down to the university looking for a teacher. Why?"

"You didn't apply for it before that?"

"No, I—"

"Are you adopted?"

Jolene took a step back, her heart a thunder in her chest. "Tell me what's going on."

"You *were* adopted?"

"My mother was a teenager. She couldn't keep me." The words tumbled out. "Why are you asking me this?"

"Because I've been trying to understand why someone is sending you the murder story," Dulcie said.

"I know it doesn't make any sense."

"It didn't—until I realized that the person writing it has just been waiting for me to inherit Laura Beaumont's property and return to Montana and find Angel Beaumont."

Jolene stared at her, eyes widening. "*You're* Angel Beaumont?"

"No," Dulcie said, shaking her head as she reached to take Jolene's hand. "*You* are."

The words barely registered as Dulcie led her to the tiny headstone next to Laura Beaumont's. An angel had been carved into the granite with the child's name cut in the wings: Angel Beaumont.

But it was the smaller letters carved in the bottom that squeezed Jolene's heart like a fist: June 5, 1980–May 11, 1985.

June 5, 1980. Jolene's birthday.

Chapter Eleven

Jolene felt numb. This was so surreal. She shook her head. "No, you're wrong." She felt faint, the heat so intense, she thought she might have to sit down.

Dulcie pulled her over into the shade of a large tree. "I'm sorry you had to learn it this way. I'm sorry we both did. But Laura Beaumont had *two* daughters," she said, taking both her hands in hers. "Do you hear me? *Two* daughters. Dulcie Ann born in 1981 and Angel Lee born in 1980. We're *sisters*."

Jolene stared at the stranger standing in front of her. She heard the words but they didn't register. She and Dulcie were sisters? "That's not possible."

"I know this is hard to believe. I'm having the same trouble, but it's true." Dulcie went on to talk about a locket and grandparents and secrets. Jolene listened but felt no connection to the people Dulcie was telling her about.

"Jolene, you *are* Angel," Dulcie said when she'd finished.

She was Angel Beaumont? The daughter of Laura Beaumont? The little girl who'd witnessed her mother's murder? The little girl someone had saved?

She shook her head and pulled her hands free. "There's been a mistake."

Dulcie studied her for a moment. "There's one way

to prove it. We can have Russell's brother at the sheriff's department run DNA tests. Then will you believe me?"

The sooner they cleared this up the better, Jolene thought, just wanting to leave the cemetery and go home. Since she was a little girl she'd always lost herself in books and that was what she wanted to do right now—curl up with a book, forget about all of this.

"Don't you see, this is why you're getting the murder story," Dulcie said. "Someone knows who you really are."

Jolene felt herself surface as if she'd been swimming up from the bottom of a deep, dark pool. "The killer's wrong." She felt her first pulse of panic. "If the killer thinks I'm Angel…"

Dulcie's expression softened. "Don't worry. I won't let anything happen to you." She smiled. "I always wanted a sister. I used to have an imaginary friend, at least that's what my parents told me it was. Her name was Angel. Don't you see? I remembered you."

Jolene brushed at the sudden tears that flooded her eyes. "It isn't that I don't believe you…"

"It's okay," Dulcie said, putting an arm around her for a moment. "Are you going to be all right?"

Jolene nodded, although she wasn't sure of that at all. "If what you're saying is true, why can't I remember? Why was none of this familiar like it was for you?"

"I suppose you repressed it because you couldn't handle what you saw. You were so young." Tears filled Dulcie's eyes again. "I'm so sorry."

Was that what she'd done? Buried the memory? "You think that's why I came back here? Why I took this job?"

"Maybe."

She studied Dulcie. *Her sister?* "What if the killer got me back here?"

"Let's not jump to conclusions."

"Jump to conclusions?" Jolene cried. "One minute you're telling me you're Angel. The next you're telling me I am." She shook her head and stepped back. Her life had always been dull. Older parents. No siblings. Her only friends on the isolated farm where she lived were the animals and the characters in the stacks of books she read. Was it any surprise she wanted to believe this was fiction?

"It's going to be all right," Dulcie said, trying to comfort her.

But Jolene knew better.

DULCIE WASN'T SURE HOW she'd expected Jolene to react to the news. She'd hoped she would be as happy as she was about having a sister. She'd handled it poorly. But she'd suspected the truth the moment she'd heard Laura had two daughters.

The gravestone with Jolene's birth date on it only proved it. Angel Beaumont was alive, back in Whitehorse and someone was sending her the murder story.

That's why Dulcie had to find the killer fast.

Back at Jolene's tiny house, she watched her sister in the kitchen pouring them each a glass of tea. She understood why Jolene didn't want to believe this.

Still, she seemed too calm and Dulcie worried that Jolene didn't understand how much danger she was in. Or didn't want to face it, the same way she didn't want to believe she was Angel.

They'd said little after they'd left the cemetery and driven into town to the sheriff's office. Shane had taken

DNA from each of them and promised to put a rush on the results, then they'd come back to Jolene's house.

Dulcie knew that Jolene had to have buried the memories of her first five years here in Whitehorse along with the murder of their mother. "Maybe you should talk to someone. A health care professional who's dealt with this sort of thing before."

"A psychiatrist?" Jolene shook her head. "Let's just wait for the DNA test results, okay? Because you're wrong."

Unfortunately, the results might not come soon enough, Dulcie thought. Who else knew Angel Beaumont was alive? Deputy Sheriff Shane Corbett, Russell Corbett, the person who'd saved Angel that night on the road, whoever had faked Angel's death, whoever had whisked her away to be adopted illegally to hide her from the killer, and the killer?

A lot of people knew Angel Beaumont was alive. But how many knew Jolene Stevens was Angel?

"You can't stay here," Dulcie said. "It's too dangerous." She couldn't bear the thought of finding a sister she never knew she had only to lose her.

Jolene handed her a glass of tea and plopped down on the couch in front of the fan. The hot air lifted the russet hair that had escaped her ponytail. Dulcie saw with clarity that her older sister's hair was a shade darker than her own.

"I *have* to stay here. If I leave, the killer won't give me the ending of the story."

"You already *know* the ending," Dulcie cried.

"No, I don't. There is so much I don't know. If I'm who you say I am, then I don't know why our mother was killed. I don't know who saved me. I don't know who it is I have to fear."

Dulcie couldn't believe this. "You think the killer is going to confess all to you?"

"I do. Why else give me the other parts of the story? He—or she—wants me to *understand*."

Dulcie was shaking her head. "It's too dangerous. The killer can't let you live once you know, don't you see that?"

"I've made up my mind. The killer won't act until he's finished the story. He wouldn't kill me before then."

"There is just one flaw in your logic. What if the killer isn't writing the story?"

"He is. No one else knows what happened that day but the killer."

And Jolene, Dulcie thought with a shudder. But she could see her sister wasn't going to change her mind. At least Jolene wasn't completely denying that she was Angel and she seemed to have pulled herself together. "I swear you're as stubborn as—"

"You?"

She stared at Jolene for a moment then began to laugh. "We *are* sisters. You'll see. That's why you can't expect me to sit back and wait all weekend."

"I didn't expect you would, knowing you just the short time I have."

"We have to find the killer before you get the last of the murder story," Dulcie said, with renewed determination. She pulled a pad and pen from her purse and began making a list of what they did know.

"Midge Atkinson befriended Laura, then her husband had an affair with Laura. Both definitely suspects. Midge should also know who the friend was who Angel played with at the creek. Also there is the rainmaker and a man named Ben Carpenter who knew Laura." She looked up. Jolene had an odd expression on her face. "Is something wrong?"

"No."

"It's not much, but at least it's a place to start, right?"

"I still think the answer is in the murder story."

"We've both read it a dozen times—"

"I'm going to read it again. There has to be something in it that points to the killer."

Dulcie studied her sister. "If you're that sure the person writing the story is the killer, then maybe we should turn the story over to the sheriff."

Jolene was shaking her head. "The story isn't over. The killer will finish it if we just wait."

But finish it how?

"Monday I'll get the end of the story. In the meantime..." Jolene glanced toward the table. "I need to return that basket to Midge Atkinson. Maybe we could do it tomorrow? I'm really tired today and I want to reread the murder story. I'll be fine here alone. I need to be alone, okay?"

Dulcie knew she had little choice. Jolene was determined that the killer wanted her to read the ending and that she would be safe until then.

She just hoped Jolene was right and they had until Monday morning to find the killer.

"I NEED YOUR HELP."

Russell couldn't believe his ears. He'd spent an afternoon in hell, worrying about Dulcie. Just the sound of her voice on the phone made his heart lift like helium.

"You know you have my help. What can I do? Did I mention I'm glad you called?"

He heard her chuckle on the other end of the line. "Meet me in town at my motel?"

"I'll see you in fifteen minutes, ten if you need me there sooner."

She laughed. "Fifteen will be fine."

Russell wavered between being relieved that she'd finally asked for his help—and worried, since he knew what it would take for her to ask.

This was about Laura Beaumont's killer, he was sure of that. The killer had stayed hidden for twenty-four years. Did Dulcie really think she could flush him out?

Of course she did. And she would, if humanly possible, and no matter the consequence. That, he knew, was what terrified him. He couldn't bear the thought of losing her.

That thought made him laugh. He would lose her to Chicago even if he could keep her from getting herself killed here in Whitehorse. It was just a matter of time until Dulcie left. She was a city girl, after all. He could already feel the hole she would leave in his life.

It was crazy how she'd gotten under his skin. All these years, he'd barely dated. He met women, but none of them could hold his interest. Then again, none of them had been Dulcie Hughes.

What if the killer *was* still around? And worse, what if he'd had help concealing his crime? Maybe not help from the entire community as Dulcie suspected, but from someone close to him. Someone as determined as the killer to keep the secret.

As he pulled up in front of the motel fifteen minutes later, Dulcie came out and slid into the passenger side of his truck. "Thanks for coming."

His heart did a little Texas two-step at just the sight of her. "How are you?"

"Fine." The lie seemed to freeze on her lips. "There's something I need to tell you. Angel Beaumont isn't dead."

He listened in shock as she told him about Jolene Stevens and handed him what she said was a copy of a short story the teacher believed the killer had been writing for her.

"You need to take this to my brother at the sheriff's department," he said when he finished reading it.

"No. And neither can you. I promised Jolene. Shane knows about Angel. He's getting DNA tests run for us."

"Do you realize how dangerous this is, not just for you, but for your sister?" He saw her expression and quickly backed off. "All right. But you need help."

She smiled. "That's why I called you. I know you haven't been here long, but you know more people than I do. I have to find the killer before Monday morning. Will you help me?"

He'd move heaven and earth for this woman if possible. "Do you have something in mind?"

"We need to know who was in Laura Beaumont's life."

He noticed that she hadn't said "her mother's life." "Okay."

"The problem is no one will talk to me about it."

He wasn't sure anyone would talk to him either, but he couldn't let her down. He started the pickup and headed toward downtown Whitehorse.

JOLENE SAT DOWN WITH the murder story, but she couldn't concentrate and finally put it away and walked to the window to stare out at the landscape. The late-afternoon sun hung at the edge of the horizon, gilding the dry grasses with its golden light.

The rolling prairie, with the Little Rockies dark and constant against the horizon, had brought her a sense of peace. How was that possible, given the horror of what she must have seen when she'd lived here?

And why hadn't she started remembering? Was the truth buried so deep that even coming back here hadn't triggered it?

She shook her head, reminding herself that she didn't believe she was Angel Beaumont. Or did she?

Dulcie believed it and so did the killer, apparently. But why the story? Was he afraid she would remember someday and, upon hearing about the writing assignment, had decided to tell her his side of the story?

Was it possible that for twenty-four years the members of this community had lived with a murderer in their midst? Had they protected the killer the same way they'd protected her years ago? Who, she wondered, had saved her that day? Not just saved her, but found a couple willing to adopt her—illegally.

Her parents had explained to her that they couldn't adopt through normal channels because of their advanced ages.

Like Dulcie's parents, Jolene's were also gone. She'd lost her father first four years ago, then her mother passed away while she was still in college. There would be no answers coming from them.

Someone in this community knew though and as her gaze took in the vehicles parked outside the community center, Jolene told herself that this time someone in the Whitehorse Sewing Circle was going to tell her.

WHEN RUSSELL ARRIVED in town, he'd made the acquaintance of Bridger and Laci Duvall. The two owned the Northern Lights restaurant and had recently had a baby boy.

Laci had been born and raised here so it was her Russell hoped to talk to when he pulled up in front of the restaurant.

He knew one of the Duvalls would be there cooking something for the supper crowd that evening and lucked out when he found Laci sliding a batch of her flourless chocolate cake into the oven.

"Russell," she said, giving him a kiss on the cheek. "I see you survived the wedding."

"Barely," he admitted. Three of his brothers had recently wed in a triple ceremony that wouldn't soon be forgotten in Whitehorse. Laci and her husband had catered it.

"Only two Corbett bachelors left," she said with an exaggerated sigh.

"Don't start," he warned playfully, then introduced her to Dulcie and told her what they needed.

"I know how people here are about their secrets, especially in Old Town Whitehorse." Laci thought for a moment then smiled broadly. "I know just the person. Her name is Nina Mae Cross and you can find her at the rest home. I should warn you. She's a little irascible."

JOLENE PUSHED OPEN THE door to the Whitehorse Community Center and stepped inside. It felt cooler in here in the large, dim, shadowy room. At the back, all of the quilters turned to see who had come in—just as they had last time.

Only this time, no one looked pleased to see her.

She walked to the back where they were gathered over the same small quilt they'd been working on the other day. She hadn't paid much attention then, but she did remember the small squares of bright colors. Today the women seemed to be embroidering tiny flowers along the edge of the baby quilt.

"Did you change your mind about learning to quilt?" Pearl Cavanaugh asked, looking hopeful.

"No," Jolene said. "I changed my mind about letting you get away without telling me about Laura Beaumont. I want to know what really happened to her daughter."

The room was instantly, deathly quiet.

Pearl put down her needle and thread. There was a trembling in her hands as she reached for her cane. "I don't believe you've ever seen our kitchen," she said, pushing herself up.

Jolene stepped back to let her lead the way and followed, afraid at how unsteady Pearl seemed on her feet.

They passed through a doorway. "Close the door behind you," Pearl said over her shoulder.

Jolene did as she was told, noticing that the other women were staring after them, but none had moved.

Suddenly Pearl turned to face her and Jolene saw that she was furious.

"What has possessed you to come in here and demand—"

"I have *every* right if I'm Angel Beaumont."

The rest of Pearl's words died on her lips.

"I am, aren't I?" The words came out a whisper.

Pearl leaned into her cane, swaying slightly. She took a step toward one of the chairs next to a small table and dropped into it.

As Jolene stared at the woman, she thought of the baby quilt the women were making—and the tiny embroidered flowers along the edge—and had to sit down in one of the chairs herself.

"I have a quilt like that one out there you're making,"

she said, her voice breaking. The Whitehorse Sewing Circle had made her a quilt when she was a baby? Or when she'd been secreted away and adopted by parents in Seattle?

"You didn't know when I got the teaching job that I was Angel?"

Pearl shook her head. "The name was Thompson."

Why hadn't Jolene thought of it? Her adopted father had died when she was six. Her mother, Marie Thompson, had remarried and changed her name. Larry Stevens had adopted her.

Pearl met her gaze and Jolene saw the compassion in those pale blue eyes. She felt tears burn her own eyes.

"You can't stay here. It isn't safe."

"It never was safe, since I believe my mother's killer is the one who got me back here." She brushed away her tears, angry that so many people had lied to her. She didn't need a DNA test. She'd seen the truth in Pearl's face. "Have you been protecting my mother's killer?"

"Of course not," Pearl snapped.

Jolene got to her feet. "You must have had your suspicions twenty-four years ago about who murdered her. Or maybe I told you."

"You weren't…talking. You didn't talk for months afterward. I don't know who was responsible and I'm certainly not going to speculate."

"But you do know who found me that night on the road."

Pearl's gaze widened. "You remember being found on the road. If you're starting to remember—"

"Just tell me who found me."

NINA MAE CROSS WAS A tiny gray-haired woman with twinkling blue eyes and dimples. Russell had been warned that Nina Mae was tough as nails and quite outspoken.

But he hadn't been ready for this little waif of a woman.

"Nina Mae Cross?"

"Who wants to know?" the wiry little woman asked, one hand on her hip as she stood in the middle of her room.

"My name's Russell Corbett."

"Never heard of you." She started to turn away.

"But you have heard of Laura Beaumont."

She stopped and turned back toward him, eyes narrowing. "Everyone's heard of that one," she said.

"Mind if we sit down? This is my friend Dulcie Hughes."

"Never heard of her either," Nina Mae said but waved them into the two available chairs. She lowered herself to the edge of the bed and looked from one to the other with an intent gaze. "Friends, huh?" She chuckled.

"Can you tell us about Laura Beaumont?" Dulcie asked.

"What's to tell? She's dead."

"We're trying to find out who killed her," Russell said. "You have any ideas?"

"Lots of ideas. Could have been a jealous wife. Could have been a jealous lover."

"Like John Atkinson?" Dulcie asked, lowering her voice.

Nina Mae smiled sagely. "So you already know about John. He'll be doing whatever Midge says till his dying day." She shook her head as if she couldn't imagine anything worse.

"What about Ben Carpenter, John's ranch manager? Was he one of the men?"

"John thought so. He fired Ben, sent him packing.

Couldn't have been a worse time with Ronda pregnant and then when she lost the baby…" Nina Mae wagged her head sympathetically. "Ben had wanted that baby so bad. It changed him for the worse, Ronda losing that baby. Ronda had her son from her first marriage, Tinker, but Ben and the boy never got along."

"I heard Laura's little girl played with a friend at the creek. Was it Tinker?" Dulcie asked, her heart in her throat.

Nina Mae nodded.

Tinker, the friend. The boy who'd tried to protect her. And the cowboy Dulcie had seen her with at the restaurant. Did he know Jolene was Angel? Is that why he'd asked her out?

"Tinker took that little girl's death hard. Before that he'd been such a good boy, but after, he was in trouble all the time. Before that, he idolized Ben. After…" She shook her head. "There was a time I thought the two of them would kill each other."

Tinker and his stepfather? "That must have been hard on Tinker's mother, Ronda," Dulcie said.

"Ronda loved Ben and stuck by him although I wouldn't have," Nina Mae said.

"We've heard that Laura might have fallen in love and was breaking it off with the others," Dulcie said.

Nina Mae's sharp eyes shone. "Funny you should say that. I heard talk that it was John, but I always figured it had to be Ben. Then again it was that hot, dry spring so that rainmaker…"

"That's quite enough," snapped an elderly woman from the doorway.

Dulcie turned at the shuffling sound to see a handsome woman leaning on her cane and understood at once why her voice had sounded odd. She'd had a stroke at some point. One side of her face hung lower than the other.

"You've said quite enough, dear," the woman said to Nina Mae more kindly. "Perhaps you'd like to go down to the nurses' station for some juice."

"Juice?" Nina Mae bristled. "I'd rather have a beer." But she rose and left anyway.

"She won't remember what she was going for by the time she reaches the nurses' station. I'm Pearl Cavanaugh." She said it as if the name should mean something to them.

Clearly someone at the nursing home had alerted Pearl about Nina Mae's company. She must have raced right in to make sure Nina Mae didn't spill the beans.

"You're one of those Corbett men," Pearl said, nodding to herself. "I heard you were all handsome, but clearly that was an understatement. What are you doing bothering Nina Mae? Didn't anyone tell you she has Alzheimer's? You can't believe anything she says."

"Can't we?" Dulcie asked, wondering how long Pearl had stood outside the room listening.

Pearl turned to scrutinize her. "You must be the woman who bought the old Beaumont place."

Dulcie had heard about Pearl and Titus Cavanaugh from Jolene. They were like royalty in Old Town Whitehorse, running everything from the school to the Whitehorse Sewing Circle. If anyone knew the truth about Laura Beaumont's murder, it was this woman.

"Actually, I *inherited* the Beaumont place." Dulcie couldn't miss the surprise in the woman's eyes and then the realization of who she was. "I'm Dulcie Hughes, but then I suspect you know that and a whole lot more."

Chapter Twelve

Midge Atkinson opened the door and looked surprised to see that Jolene wasn't alone.

"I brought your wicker basket back," Jolene said when Midge made no move to invite her and Dulcie inside. "I brought a friend, too."

"I see that." Midge was a large-framed, thick woman, shapeless in a purple sweatsuit, her face set in a permanent scowl. "Well, come in, then." She reached for the basket, stepping back with obvious irritation.

Dulcie and Jolene followed her into the kitchen. After her run-in with Pearl Cavanaugh the day before, Dulcie didn't expect Midge Atkinson to be any more forthcoming that Pearl had been.

"I like your borders," Dulcie said. "Did you paint them?"

"Yes," Midge said as she put the wicker basket on the top shelf and turned toward them. "But you aren't here to return my basket or compliment my artwork. What do you want?"

Clearly word had spread about the Beaumont girls. "We're here to ask you about Laura Beaumont," Dulcie said.

Midge swung her gaze to Jolene. "I warned you about

digging into things that don't concern you. If you care about your teaching job—"

"Actually, it does concern us and I think you know it," Dulcie cut in. "We know you painted Angel Beaumont's room and that you were friends with Laura Beaumont."

"I want you both to leave. *Now*." Midge started to take a step toward the phone as if to call for help, when Jolene finally spoke.

"You were the one who saved Angel that night."

All the air seemed to be sucked from the room. Midge swung around, almost lost her balance and had to grab the countertop to keep from falling.

Dulcie also turned in shock to look at Jolene. Why hadn't Jolene told her this?

Midge looked as if she might have a heart attack right in front of their eyes. She stumbled to the table and sat down heavily in one of the chairs. "Who told you that I—"

"It doesn't matter," Jolene said, sounding calm as she took a seat and Dulcie did the same.

Midge was staring at Jolene. So Midge really hadn't suspected that Jolene was Angel?

"Were you also responsible for me coming back here?" Jolene asked.

"A committee of parents was involved in the hiring," Midge said. "I don't know who suggested you. I didn't know…"

"Why were you on that road that night?" Dulcie asked.

"I went there looking for John," Midge said in a tiny voice. "His pickup wasn't there."

"You must have seen the killer."

Midge shook her head. "All I saw was Angel. I started to go toward the house, but I couldn't leave the girl. I could see that something horrible had happened. She had blood all over her." Her voice broke. "I got out of there. I took the girl and went home. John was there. He'd been there the whole time cleaning so we could move into the house."

"He hadn't just gotten back from Laura's?" Dulcie asked.

"He hadn't been near Laura's. I checked his truck. The engine was ice-cold. He told me she'd broken it off with him, said she'd fallen in love."

"With Ben Carpenter?" Dulcie asked.

Midge pursed her lips. "That's what I heard."

"You were the one who put the note on my car, weren't you?" Jolene said.

Midge looked embarrassed. "I was trying to protect you."

"Or protect yourself?" Dulcie said.

Jolene rose to leave. "Thank you," she said to Midge and started toward the door.

"That's it?" Dulcie said when she caught up to her sister outside Midge's house.

"I'm sorry I didn't tell you what I'd discovered," Jolene said. "Midge found me. She got Angel…me to some people who located a couple interested in adopting me illegally. It's still a shock and it's going to take me a while to…"

"It's okay," Dulcie said, understanding. They were strangers. Sisters, but strangers. In time maybe…

They turned as Midge came out of the house. "You want to know who killed Laura?" She sounded angry. "Ask Ronda Carpenter. But don't let that timid act of hers fool you. That woman is capable of murder. She and Laura were the best of friends until she lost her baby." Midge seemed glad to finally unburden herself of this news. "I heard Rhonda and Ben fighting that night. Could hear them clear up at the house from that old trailer they lived in on our property. Who knows if Ben pushed her or she fell like she swore later, but she lost her baby and Laura Beaumont was dead by that evening. So you tell me who killed Laura."

With that Midge went back into the house and slammed the door.

"ARE YOU ALL RIGHT?" Dulcie asked.

"Please stop asking me that," Jolene said as Dulcie drove them away from the Atkinson Ranch. "I know I'm Angel Beaumont, but still, it's as if everyone is talking about someone else."

"I only asked because it's hard for me to hear these things about our mother," Dulcie said, her eyes on the road. "I thought it might be for you, too."

Jolene stared out the window. "I want to go by her house."

Dulcie shot her a look. "I don't think that's a good idea."

"I have to see it. You said yourself that we need to find the killer. If I saw him that day, going to the house might make me remember."

"You don't know what kind of reaction you might have."

"If you don't take me, then I'll go alone."

They drove in silence to the old farmhouse. As Dulcie pulled up in front, she let out a curse. "I locked that door," she said, cutting the engine. "Someone keeps leaving it open. Don't you dare say ghosts."

Jolene wasn't about to say it but if there were ghosts, then they would most assuredly be in this house, she told herself as she got out.

The house loomed in front of her. She stood, waiting to feel something, some sense of having been here before, to hit her like a brick, to make her remember.

She could feel Dulcie watching her expectantly as she walked toward the house. At the front door, she hesitated, some of her courage deserting her.

"You don't have to do this," Dulcie said at her side.

Jolene stepped in and grimaced at the smell, but was determined not to let Dulcie see how truly afraid she was.

As she walked through the living room toward the back of the house, she expected any moment to see something that would send her into some kind of shock.

She found the kitchen at the back. On the table were a bowl and spoon, a small plate and butter knife. Her last meal with her mother?

She tried to imagine herself sitting there. Tried to imagine the woman sitting across from her. Her mother.

"Jolene?" Dulcie asked behind her.

She shook her head as she moved away from the table and headed for the stairs. Might as well get it over with.

"Honey, I'm not sure—"

Jolene didn't wait to hear what Dulcie had to say. She'd come this far. She had to go upstairs. Part of her prayed that she would remember. She wanted these people to mean something to her. Laura Beaumont. Angel Beaumont. Dulcie, the sister she never knew she had.

As she hurried up the stairs, her heart a-thunder in her chest, she heard Dulcie at her heels.

At the top of the stairs, Jolene slowed. All her senses were on alert as she turned. One room caught her eye.

A child's room. Angels painted on the walls. They were as striking as Dulcie had said they were.

She moved toward the room like a sleepwalker. Angel Beaumont's room. *Her* room. At the door she stopped and was surprised when she burst into tears. She felt Dulcie's hand on her shoulder.

"Jolene? Do you *remember?*"

She shook her head. "I just suddenly felt so sorry for this little girl," she said, wiping her tears. "There is so much sadness in this room. Loneliness. Can't you feel it?"

Dulcie nodded.

"Where is her room?" She couldn't bring herself to call Laura her mother. And yet calling her Laura felt wrong, too.

"Down there."

Jolene walked toward the open door to the room at the front of the house. She could see part of a faded yellow curtain billowing in and out on the hot wind.

Jolene had to force herself, one foot in front of the other, to enter the room. The vanity against the wall, the dresser... She froze as she saw the stained bed. The murder story leaped into her mind and she could see the woman lying on the bed, the killer standing over her, the glint of the knife's blade in the light.

After a moment she let the breath out she'd been holding. She could feel Dulcie's gaze on her, a look of fear and wonder in her eyes—and hope.

She felt nothing. Even when she told herself that her mother had died here. She couldn't remember that mother, couldn't remember this life at all. Thank God.

"Sorry," she said to Dulcie as she turned and left the room.

"Nothing at all?" Dulcie asked as they descended the stairs.

"Nothing." Jolene was surprised how relieved she felt. She'd been terrified of what she might remember and how she would react. Now she just felt empty as she and Dulcie left the house.

At the car, Jolene heard a sound that made her turn and look back. The weather vane on the barn groaned in the wind. Just like the one her adoptive father used to have on his barn—before he had it taken down.

"I think we'd better go see Ronda Carpenter."

"SON?"

Dragged from his thoughts, Russell turned to find his father standing at the edge of his cabin porch. He'd been mentally kicking himself and hadn't heard him approach.

After seeing Nina Mae yesterday, Dulcie had been upset. He'd tried his damnedest to get her to come stay out at the ranch, but she'd refused.

"I need to be alone for a while," she'd said. "Truthfully, I have trouble thinking when you're around." She'd smiled that incredible smile that made his knees weak and kissed him before shoving him out the door.

He'd known it was the best thing she could have done. If he'd stayed there in the motel room with her…

"I was hoping we could talk before supper," Grayson said, taking one of the porch chairs beside him.

Russell saw the lines of worry etched in his father's face and felt a stab of guilt. Of course his father was worried. He'd gone along with the other ranchers and farmers in hiring the rainmaker. And now…

"I'm sorry, I said I'd talk to the rainmaker…" Russell

swore. He'd been so involved with Dulcie that he hadn't given the rainmaker or rain a thought.

"The ranchers and farmers are losing their patience," Grayson said. "If this rainmaker doesn't have some results soon I'm afraid what some of the hotheads of the bunch might do, true enough. But that isn't what I wanted to speak to you about."

Russell hadn't been on the ranch much either the past few days. "Is something going on I should know about?"

"That would be my question," Grayson said.

"I'm sorry. I've been involved in… Dulcie, the woman I brought to dinner, she found out that she's one of Laura Beaumont's daughters. Now she's more determined than ever to find the person who killed her mother."

"She's a lovely, intelligent, determined woman. I can understand why you're concerned about her. Surely your brother is looking into this."

"Shane's doing his best since the sheriff is out of town, but the trail is twenty-four years old and the community isn't talking."

His father raised a brow. "You think the community is protecting the killer?"

"Maybe. Someone tried to run Dulcie off the road. Shane says he doesn't think it's connected."

"But you do."

Russell nodded. "I've tried to reason with her."

His father chuckled, then turned serious. "You care a lot about this woman."

Russell realized now what was bothering his father. "I would never leave the ranch."

Grayson smiled ruefully. "Love makes a man do things he swears he never would."

"Can you imagine me in Chicago?" He shook his

head. "No matter how I feel about her, nothing will get me away from Trails West Ranch." Even as he said the words, Russell realized that Dulcie had *already* gotten him away from the ranch. All his thoughts for days had been about her and only her.

AT THE RURAL MAILBOX with the word *Carpenter* crudely printed on the side of the rusted metal, Dulcie turned off the dirt road and into the yard of the run-down farmhouse.

Two mongrel dogs came charging out, barking. As she cut the engine, she looked over at Jolene, who also was debating whether to get out with both large dogs barking wildly just outside the car.

The front door of the house swung open. Ronda Carpenter called off the dogs, frowning, as Jolene got out of the car. Her frown deepened when she saw Dulcie.

Ronda was one of those tiny women, small-boned, late forties and beat-down looking. Jolene had seen her only once before. At her interview for the teaching job. Ronda had been on the parent committee that recommended hiring her.

"If this is about Mace he isn't here," Ronda called. "He and his father went to Havre. Is he in trouble?"

"No," Jolene said. "Mace's fine."

Ronda looked relieved but not much. "If you're here about money for the school or something…"

"I'm not. Could we step in out of the heat for a few moments?"

Ronda looked worried as Jolene and Dulcie followed her up the steps and into her kitchen. "I need to get supper made. Ben and Mace will be back soon. I hope this won't take long."

Jolene stood for a moment watching the woman's trembling hands as she put some water on to boil, took out a large bag of elbow macaroni, a can of cream of mushroom soup and two cans of tuna. Dulcie was glancing around the old farmhouse, seeing, Jolene was sure, the tattered furnishings.

"I need to ask you about Laura Beaumont," Jolene said.

Ronda froze. Slowly she put down the can opener she'd been using on the tuna-fish cans.

"I heard she was a friend of yours," Jolene said. "I was hoping you could tell me a little about her."

Ronda didn't turn around. "That was so long ago. Why would you care about—"

"It's important or we wouldn't come here and ask you questions that might upset you," Jolene said. "We need to know what Ben's relationship was with Laura."

"What?" Ronda clutched the edge of the counter.

"What she's asking is if Ben was having an affair with Laura," Dulcie said and shrugged when Jolene shot her a warning look.

"No. Ben? No." Ronda turned around. She looked sick. "Who are you?"

"I'm sorry," Jolene said. "This is Dulcie Hughes. She owns the old Beaumont place."

Ronda's gaze swung to Dulcie, her eyes widening.

"I'm sorry, but we have to ask you these questions," Jolene said. "Midge Atkinson told us that her husband fired Ben because he was having an affair with Laura."

"John was *wrong*. He was the one—" Ronda clutched the apron material tied at her waist in both fists. "Ben was never with Laura. She was *my* friend. You have it all wrong."

"Then help us," Jolene said.

She was shaking her head, her eyes dull with pain. "Please, you both need to leave now."

"I know Tinker tried to protect Angel Beaumont the day her mother died," Jolene said.

"Tinker?" Ronda's gaze cleared. Anger shone in her eyes. "You leave my Tinker alone, you hear me?" She picked up the can opener from the counter and advanced on them as if she meant to strike them. "Get out and don't you come back. If Ben catches you here…"

Jolene took a step back and Dulcie was already headed for the door when they heard a vehicle coming up the road.

"Go," Ronda cried. "If Ben finds you here, he'll think it's about Mace. He doesn't want Mace turning out like his stepbrother."

Dulcie opened the door and they both stepped out on the porch as a truck drove past but didn't stop.

Ronda stood in the doorway, hanging on to the knob as if her relief had turned her knees to water. Just before she slammed the door, Jolene saw the hateful look she shot the two of them.

As the sound of the door slamming died off, Jolene thought she heard someone sobbing on the other side. Huge racking sobs that tore at Jolene's heart. How many lives had Laura Beaumont destroyed before losing her own?

"What do you make of that?" Dulcie asked once they were in the car and far enough away there was no chance of running into Ben Carpenter.

"I think Ronda is afraid of her husband," Jolene said.

"Then why is she still with him after everything he's done to her? I told you what Nina Mae Cross said about the fight Ronda and Ben had and Ronda losing the baby after a fall. You know the bastard pushed her, just as you know he was having an affair with Laura."

"Maybe there's more to the story." Jolene hoped so. "We'll know in the morning," she said with a sigh.

Dulcie glanced over at her. "You can't still expect the end of the murder story? Jolene, if the killer is writing it, then he knows what we've been up to. You don't still think he—"

"The killer will finish because he wants me to know why he killed Laura," Jolene said.

Dulcie was shaking her head. "Why is he going to confess? We are no closer to finding out who killed Laura than when we both arrived in town. The killer has no reason to give himself—or herself—up. Not after twenty-four years. There isn't going to be any more short story. You have to face the fact that we may never know the truth."

RUSSELL LOOKED UP as Dulcie made her way to his table at Northern Lights restaurant. When he'd called earlier to see if she would have dinner with him, she'd sounded discouraged. Now as she walked toward the table, he could see it in her face.

"Bad day?" he asked as he rose to help her with her chair.

There were dark circles under her eyes and she looked as if she carried the weight of the world on her shoulders.

"I feel as if I'm beating my head against a wall." She filled him in on the talk with Midge Atkinson and Ronda Horton Carpenter as well as what Jolene had found out.

"I think Ronda Carpenter is in major denial but

after meeting her husband, Ben, I can't imagine how my mother could have been in love with him."

"Nina Mae said he changed after the loss of his baby," Russell reminded her. "If he and your mother were truly in love, her death must have changed him, as well."

"Of course there is always the chance that Midge is lying, and John was the man my mother was in love with and Ben was the man who got dumped."

"I see why you feel like you're beating your head against a wall," Russell said.

"That's just it. We have no idea who is lying and who is telling the truth. On top of that, Ben's son, Mace, is one of Jolene's students and Jolene has been going out with Ben's stepson, Tinker. What a tangled mess."

"Small-town Montana," Russell said.

"Do you think Tinker knows who Jolene really is?"

Russell shrugged. "I wouldn't worry about it, though. Didn't he try to protect her when they were kids?"

"Yes." She rubbed her temples. "Give me some good news. What did you find out about my mother's locket?"

Russell wished he had good news. "The locket wasn't on the body, according to the coroner's report."

"Are you telling me the killer took it?"

"Or it was misplaced during the investigation. I'm sorry. Shane got the DNA reports back." Russell nodded. "You and Jolene are sisters."

"Does Jolene—"

"She knows. Shane just let me know. He said she took the news fine. Sounds as if she's accepting that part of it at least."

Dulcie shook her head. "I don't like Jolene out there alone. I wanted to stay with her. I even offered to put her up at the same motel where I'm staying. I'm worried about her."

"I'm worried about *you*." He met her gaze. All he wanted was to take her in his arms and comfort her. They hadn't made love since that one and only time at the old farmhouse and that hadn't been his idea of making love.

He wanted to get this woman in a proper bed and make love to her the way she deserved. He leaned toward her and said as much.

She gave him a broad smile, light shining in her dark eyes, along with a challenge. "So what's stopping you?"

"I want your undivided attention." He wanted more than that, but he was smart enough not to voice it. He got the impression she wanted this to be casual. He didn't do casual.

She sobered and looked toward the bank of dark windows. "I can't give you what you want right now."

"I know," he said. "So what now?"

"We wait and see if the killer finishes the murder story," Dulcie said. "Or did you mean with me and you?"

AFTER DULCIE LEFT RUSSELL in the parking lot by the restaurant with little more than a brief kiss, she felt restless. She'd hoped he would change his mind and come back with her to the motel.

But she understood how he felt. He was the kind of man who fell hard when he fell for a woman. He was afraid of falling for her and with good reason.

She knew she wasn't going to be able to sleep. Just as she knew that she'd purposely let herself be distracted with Laura Beaumont's murder. She didn't want to think about what her grandparents had done.

Nor did she want to examine too closely how she felt about Russell Corbett.

Back at her motel, she thought about the farmhouse because it was easier than thinking about the rest of it right now. The house hadn't been broken into, which meant someone had a key.

Laura Beaumont had given someone a key to her place? The man she'd fallen in love with, Dulcie thought with a start.

It made perfect sense if what the writer of the murder story and Midge had told them was true. Laura had fallen in love. She'd broken it off with the other men, which explained that scene in the murder story where one of the men was arguing with Laura in the bathroom. John Atkinson? Ben Carpenter? The rainmaker? Or had there been others that even the storyteller hadn't known about?

Excited that she might have stumbled onto something, Dulcie changed her clothes, dressed for a long night of it, and equipped with water, a flashlight and pepper spray, drove toward the farmhouse. Tonight she would find out who Laura had given a key to. Find out who the man was that Laura had fallen in love with.

Dulcie was putting her money on Ben Carpenter. That was the reason she'd brought the pepper spray. The man scared her.

On the drive to the farmhouse, she debated calling Russell until it was too late. No cell service.

She parked up the road and walked, telling herself that all the rattlesnakes had gone back under their rocks for the night. At the house, she found a spot where she could hide to wait and settled in.

An hour later she was wondering if her theory was as

ridiculous as her hiding out here when she heard a sound coming from off in the darkness. The swishing sound became recognizable. Someone was moving through the tall, dry grass toward her.

Chapter Thirteen

A black shape emerged from out of the darkness. Dulcie couldn't see a face, just a large, man-size form as he passed within feet of her. She pressed herself against the wall and didn't dare breathe until he turned the corner of the house.

She heard the clomp of his boots on the steps and across the porch, then using his key, the man entered the house.

Just as she'd thought. He *had* a key.

But who had it been? She crept around the corner of the house. He'd left the door wide-open. She could hear him climbing the stairs, his footfalls labored.

She waited until she heard nothing then she edged to the porch steps and glanced inside. Pitch darkness and putrid air filled the house.

Was she really going inside?

A light flashed on in the upstairs front bedroom, making her jump. The man was in Laura Beaumont's bedroom. The faint glow shone through the yellow curtain.

What was he doing in Laura's room? Just touching her things, remembering? Or was he searching for something? Evidence that she'd overlooked?

She debated what to do, knowing what Russell would say about her impetuous behavior. Taking the bull by the horns, so to speak, she crept up onto the porch and entered the house. She didn't dare use her flashlight. But she checked to make sure it and the pepper spray were still in her vest pockets. They were.

The blackness inside the house was complete. It made her feel dizzy, screwed up her equilibrium. She closed her eyes, envisioning where everything was as she inched to the bottom of the stairs, her hands out like a sleepwalker.

She tried not to think about what she would do if she touched flesh and blood. Listening, hearing nothing, she started up the stairs.

Five steps, stop and listen, another five. At the top, she stumbled and froze, afraid her clumsiness might have been heard.

A strange sound was coming from the front bedroom. A high keening sound like that of a wounded animal. Her blood turned to ice.

Was it the man? Who else? No one but he had gone into the house and she didn't believe in ghosts, did she?

Dulcie found the wall in the dark and worked her way carefully along it. The keening had changed to something almost more frightening, a horrible choking sound.

She moved toward the dim light and the sound, determined to get a look at the man and then run like hell.

As she reached the doorway she saw the man on his knees beside the bed. His flashlight lay on the bed, the shaft of light splashed across the room.

He was hunched over, holding something in his right hand, his body convulsing with what she realized were sobs.

The sight gripped her. She watched him, his hands balling into fists, his body quivering, choking out sobs as if bringing them up from some deep, dark well inside him.

The muscles of his right hand flexed, the fingers opening. In the light from his flashlight lying on the bed, she saw what he held. A gold locket on a chain.

Her heart stopped. All breath rushed out of her. Time seemed to freeze as her muscles turned to mush.

The man spun around so fast she didn't see the blow coming, couldn't have moved even if she had. His fist caught her on the side of the head, knocking her back into the wall. She smacked her head and felt the light sparkle as she slid down the wall and hit the floor, the lights going out completely.

RUSSELL JERKED UP OUT of a bad dream, confused for a moment where he was. It took a few seconds to realize what had awakened him. The phone.

He grabbed it up. "Hello?"

"It's Shane. I didn't want to wake Dad, but I thought you should know. I just arrested Finnegan Amherst."

The rainmaker? Russell sat up and tried to clear away the cobwebs of the dream, the remnants of sleep. He'd been dreaming about Dulcie. She'd been in trouble. He shook it off. "Why would you arrest—"

"I think you might want to come down here. I had the other deputy on duty take Dulcie Hughes to the hospital for—"

"What?" Russell was on his feet now, fear sending his heart into overdrive.

"Just for observation. I wanted Doc to look her over to make sure she didn't have a concussion."

"What the hell?" Russell swore as he snapped on a light and looked around for some clothes.

"She's all right, okay? She had a run-in with Finnegan Amherst."

"I'll kill that bastard."

"Settle down. He's behind bars and that's where he's going to stay. We picked him up as he was leaving town."

Leaving town? "That son-of-a-bitch."

"I knew you'd want to know about Dulcie. Russell? It looks as if she might have found Laura Beaumont's killer."

"The rainmaker? After I check on Dulcie, I want to see him."

"Not happening," his brother said.

"Where's the sheriff? I'll ask him."

"The sheriff's out of town. But he wouldn't let you see Finnegan Amherst either."

"I'm not going to kill him. I just want to talk to him."

"If you're thinking of beating a confession out of him, forget it. Anyway, he swears he didn't kill Laura."

"He swore he could make it rain, too."

DULCIE LOOKED UP TO SEE Russell coming through the door of her hospital room and felt her heart do a little jitterbug. Just the sight of him made her eyes fill with tears. She quickly brushed them away.

"Are you all right?" He looked both scared and relieved and angry. She didn't have to guess why.

"I'm fine. It's only a slight concussion." She smiled even though it hurt her jaw to do so.

Russell swore as he stepped to her, gently turning her head with his fingers to look at the dark bruise that ran from her cheekbone to her chin.

"It looks worse than it is," she said and saw him clamp down on his teeth, the muscles in his jaws bunching with fury.

"How in the hell…" His words ran out.

"It's a funny story," she said, making his eyes narrow. "I couldn't sleep so I decided to stake out the house. I knew someone was coming in at night and I had this idea that since whoever it was had a key, Laura must have given it to him. Which meant he had to be the man she'd fallen in love with and why she'd broken it off with the others."

"Get on to the part that's funny," he snapped.

"The rainmaker *was* the man. He used his key to get into the house. I followed him upstairs. I found him kneeling beside her bed…" She felt odd telling this part. "He was crying and I saw that he had something clutched in his hand. It was her locket."

Russell flinched. "Your mother's missing locket with the photo inside?"

"When he realized I was behind him, he spun around and…"

"He hit you."

"I blacked out for a few minutes. When I woke I heard his pickup leaving. I drove down to Arlene Evans and got her to call the sheriff's office. Then Arlene drove me in to see Shane and he insisted I come over here. End of story."

Russell glared down at her. "You went out to that house in the middle of the night, by yourself, looking for a killer."

"Actually, I was looking for her lover—not the killer."

"How could you do something so rash? So irrational? So damned dangerous and stupid?"

She bristled. "Reckless yes, dangerous as it turned out, but not irrational or stupid. I took pepper spray and I knew what I was doing."

"Did you?" His gaze went to her bruised face and she

watched as his expression softened. "Damn it, Dulcie." He stepped to her and pulled her into his arms.

She leaned her uninjured cheek against the warm, soft fabric of his shirt and breathed in his scent. She *had* been rash and reckless and a little crazed. Kind of like her feelings for this man.

"You're coming home with me until you have to leave for Chicago," he said.

"The killer is behind bars."

Russell pulled back to look into her eyes. "Exactly, and I have your undivided attention for a few days before you have to leave, right?"

She grinned even though it hurt her jaw. "You *did* promise me a horseback ride and I could use a few days of R & R." She touched his cheek. "Are you sure about this, Russ?"

He nodded and leaned down to kiss her softly on her lips. As he drew back, his gaze locked with hers and she realized just how risky this was. For the first time in her life, she felt as if she was in over her head.

JOLENE HAD AWAKENED late Sunday after a sleepless night. She'd stumbled into the bathroom to shower and stood for a long time studying her face in the mirror.

She was Angel Beaumont. She'd waited for the name to trigger a memory. Nothing. Just like her visit to the house. And to the jail, after Dulcie's call.

She'd looked at the rainmaker, seen nothing but a man who'd aged badly over the past twenty-four years, and felt not even the slightest stirring of recall.

"Give it time," Dulcie had said when she and Russell stopped by.

Word had traveled through the county about the arrest. Jolene had wanted to feel something. Relief.

Anger. Anything. But instead, she'd felt only a little sad. With the rainmaker in jail she would never get the end of the story.

She didn't mention this to Dulcie, knowing how foolish her sister would find it. Dulcie was convinced Jolene knew the ending, knew it probably better than anyone.

Deputy Sheriff Shane Corbett had called with the DNA results. Jolene had been expecting the outcome. She and Dulcie were sisters. DNA from the murder scene proved they were the daughters of Laura Beaumont.

By then, all things that Jolene had known. Still, she'd thought that when she got the DNA results she would feel that bond with Dulcie that sisters were supposed to feel. She'd hoped she would. She hadn't.

Maybe it was as simple as the fact that she didn't want to be Angel, didn't want to remember those first five years of her life or her mother's murder or what she must have seen.

She sighed now, wishing she could quit thinking about it. She'd read most of the cruelly hot afternoon, but even a good book couldn't distract her from her thoughts.

Putting down her book, she walked to the window, surprised it was getting dark. She felt restless, thought about going into town, but didn't have the energy or any reason. It was still unbearably hot, but now the breeze coming in the open window felt muggy.

She dreaded tomorrow. There would be no ending to the murder story. She would grade her students' assignments, then hand them all back, keeping copies for the promised anthology. School would let out early for the year. It would be over.

And yet it wouldn't be over for her until she remembered.

She couldn't bear to think about spending a long,

hot summer here now. But where would she go? Dulcie had talked about her coming back to Chicago with her. Jolene wasn't ready for that.

She turned away from the window. The house felt unbearably hot. Maybe she'd take a cool shower. She wandered into the bathroom and stripped down. As she stepped under the icy spray, she thought of Tinker and felt her stomach turn. He'd been the boy she'd played with at the creek, the friend who, according to the author of the murder story, tried to save her the night her mother was murdered.

As she shampooed her hair, she wondered if Tinker knew who she was, had known since the first time he'd asked her out at a Whitehorse Community Center dance.

The thought sent a chill through her. She turned up the hot water and stood under it for a few seconds.

Had Tinker known his father sneaked over to see Laura? He was nine, plenty old enough to know what was going on. Or had Ronda been telling the truth and Ben had never been Laura's lover?

Turning off the shower, Jolene rubbed her temples, feeling a headache coming on, if she kept this up. But she had to know who'd been writing the murder story.

As she pulled on a tank top, shorts and sandals, she padded back into her living room and glanced at the computer sitting on the desk in the corner.

She hadn't even turned it on since the one at the school was newer and had internet service. But hadn't Titus Cavanaugh mentioned that the two computers were networked together?

Moving to the desk, she stood for a moment, staring down at it, thinking of the murder story and what had bothered her about it. *Let me be wrong.* Slowly, she touched the on button. It took a moment for the computer to boot up.

Jolene jerked back as the murder story came up on the screen.

DO YOU REMEMBER YET?

Remember the crushing heat that night, wading in the warm creek water, the feel of the grass on your bare feet? Remember sitting on the bank whispering a secret in the dark?

You have a secret, don't you? That's why you don't want to remember that night and the sound of the weather vane groaning in the wind.

You know who killed your mother. You've always known. But you don't want to remember the blade of the knife, dripping bright red with your mother's blood, or the hand holding it.

JOLENE COVERED HER MOUTH as tears flooded her eyes. She shot out of the computer chair, stumbling back, almost falling. As if she could run away from the words on the screen.

Through the open window, she could smell rain in the air and feel the cool blowing in. She snatched up the phone and dialed Dulcie's number. There'd been enough secrets. Enough lies. She could no longer live with hers.

The call went straight to voice mail. The trees just outside the window whipped back in the wind, the branches scraping the side of the house like fingers across a blackboard. Dark shadows flickering shapelessly against the coming night.

"If you would like to leave a message…"

"Dulcie, I know. I know what happened that night.

I—" The words caught in her throat as she saw something through the thrashing branches.

There was a light on in the schoolhouse.

AFTER THEIR HORSEBACK RIDE, Dulcie soaked in the hot tub, hoping to relieve some of her aches and pains, and then showered. "Riding a horse isn't as romantic as it looks," she called from the bathroom. "Thank you for taking me, though. I loved seeing the country. It is so beautiful down in the Missouri Breaks. I see why you love it here."

When she didn't get an answer, she pulled on her clothes and, finding the bedroom empty, discovered Russell sitting in the living area reading something.

As she moved closer she was startled to see that he was reading the copy of the murder story that Jolene had given her.

The worry in his gaze as he looked up at her scared her.

"Why are you reading that?"

He set the copies aside and sighed. "What if Jolene receives the ending tomorrow at school?"

"That's not possible. The rainmaker is in jail."

"What if he isn't the one writing it?"

Hadn't she thought there might be someone else, an accomplice to the murderer who had helped him or her stay free the past twenty-four years?

But she'd discarded the theory when Finnegan Amherst had been arrested for the murder. The rainmaker was a loner, an outsider. No one in this town would have helped him.

"You're scaring me."

"I'm sorry. It's just that after reading this again…"

He met her gaze. "The writer is too intimate with what happened."

"Of course he is. The killer's the only one who knows the whole story."

"Except for Angel."

Dulcie felt her breath rush from her lungs. "You think she's writing it. That's she's always been the author."

"I think it's possible. Maybe more than possible. She repressed the past and yet she took this teaching job. What if her writing the murder story is Angel's way of dealing with her past?"

She bit her lip to hold back the tears. "What happens if she writes an ending to the murder story and it's on that empty desk in the morning where she found the others?"

"She'll know the truth," he said flatly.

Dulcie felt ice slide up her spine. "Russ, no. You can't think... She was only *five*. She couldn't—"

"I don't want to believe it either, Dulcie. But—"

"No. It was the rainmaker. He had the locket—" She felt the tears on her cheeks. Not her sister.

Her fury at her grandparents gripped her heart like a fist. How could they have left Angel behind, left her in such an awful situation? It didn't matter if Laura refused to give up Angel. They should have taken her anyway. They should never have separated her from her older sister.

"I'm going to call her," Dulcie said.

"Be careful what you say," Russell said behind her. "I'm afraid of what she might do when she remembers."

Dulcie didn't hear him as she listened to her sister's message.

JOLENE STARED AT THE LIGHT through the trees. She felt the faint push of memory. The feel of the warm creek water on her bare feet. The night pitch-black. The scorching wind carrying the scent of dust and dry grass and the smell of desperation.

Crying on the bank of the creek, rubbing her eyes with her fists, her hands as dirty as her clothing. Her stomach aching because she hadn't eaten since breakfast. A bowl of cereal.

She'd gone home for lunch, but her mother had been napping and the refrigerator was empty. Was that when she'd first gotten really scared? She'd kept telling herself that her mommy would get better.

Jolene had a flash of memory: her mother sitting across from her, talking too fast, scary happy, eyes too bright just as she'd seen her before, too many times.

"Everything is going to be all right now, sweetie. Fin is going to take us far away from here. Don't cry. He'll be your new daddy. He'll buy you things. He'll take care of us. He isn't like the others."

The memory fell over her, the weight of it stealing her breath, the pain of it making her want to curl up in a ball on the floor.

"Stop it! *Stop it!*" She couldn't think about this now. She had to get up to the schoolhouse. Stepping into the kitchen, she opened the top drawer. The butcher knife was long, the handle warm in her hand. As the blade caught the light, she flinched as if she could feel the blade cutting through flesh.

She started to put it back, repulsed, her stomach revolting as she remembered the smell of blood. Blood pooling on the once-white sheets, her mother's vacant eyes. She stumbled back from the open drawer, afraid she might black out, the knife gripped in her hand.

Fighting back the darkness that threatened to pull her

under, she stepped out the back door and, keeping the knife hidden behind her, started up the hill. She could see the light burning in the schoolhouse, knew who was waiting up there for her.

Do you remember yet?

You know who killed her. You've always known.

"JOLENE?" DULCIE GLANCED over at Russell next to her standing on the steps of the small house and knocked again on Jolene's door. The lights were on inside the house and both her car and her bike were out front.

When she didn't get an answer, Dulcie tried the door and found it unlocked. Her heart in her throat, she opened the door. *"Jolene?"*

The house looked empty. She stood rooted to the floor and Russell hurried past her to search for her sister.

Dulcie felt numb, too afraid almost to breathe, let alone help him search.

"She's not here," he said when he returned.

The house had felt empty, empty as she felt inside. She glanced at the computer sitting on a desk under the window in the corner.

"I'm going to go look for her," Russell said, heading for the door.

"Wait. I don't want you going alone. I want to check something." If Jolene had been writing the murder story, wouldn't it be on her computer?

She stepped to the desk, pulled up the chair and with trembling fingers touched the mouse. The screen lit up, the words leaping out at her.

You know who killed her. You've always known. But you don't want to remember the blade of the knife, dripping bright red with your mother's blood, or the hand holding it.

"Oh, God, Russell. It's here on the computer. At least part of it," Dulcie cried. "It looks as if she is in the middle of writing it—"

More words began to appear on the screen. "She's typing it right now from another computer. The school-house. The computers must be connected."

"There's a light on at the school," he said, opening the front door. "I'm going up there. Stay here."

Before she could stop him, he was gone, the door closing behind him. She looked down at the computer screen.

It's hard to admit, isn't it? This secret you've been keeping all these years. You wanted her dead. You wished it that night on the creek. Loving her was so hard. Sometimes you hated her.

You wanted to be with your sister, with your grandparents in their nice house your mother told you about.

Dulcie had to stop reading to rub her eyes to clear them of tears.

You wanted to be the chosen one who got to leave your mother and didn't have to listen to her crying at night and laughing with men and that horrible squeak of the bed springs when she told you to go play at the creek.

She's dead because you

Dulcie stared at the screen. Why had she stopped typing? Russell couldn't have reached the school yet.

THE NIGHT WAS BLACK. Earlier the wind had been hot and stinging. Now as Russell walked up the road, he sensed something had changed.

He looked to the west, past what was left of Old Town Whitehorse, and thought he saw something glitter behind the Little Rockies. Lightning? A low, distant rumble followed.

The air around him suddenly felt cooler, the wind in his face smelling of rain. He couldn't believe it. Rain? Finally this horrible hot, dry weather would end.

As he neared the schoolhouse, he told himself a lot of things would end tonight. The thought scared him. Dulcie and her sister had been through so much. They were strong, but were they strong enough to face this?

He glanced back, wishing now he hadn't left Dulcie alone in the house. But bringing her with him was out of the question. He had no idea what he would find at the schoolhouse.

Was there any doubt now that Jolene was the author of the murder story? Was she even aware of it? He could see that, like tonight, she might have gotten up in the middle of the night to write it and then taken the story to the schoolhouse to leave it for her conscious self to find.

How disturbed was Jolene? They'd all thought that her being unable to remember was because she'd seen her mother's murderer. But what if they'd been wrong? What if she'd killed her mother? That could explain why she'd buried the memory so deep that it could only surface as if someone else was telling the story—and why the town had banned together to protect her.

At the schoolhouse, he stopped to listen. A bolt of lightning splintered the sky; this time the answering boom of thunder followed close behind. The wind kicked up, moaning along the eaves. Closer, the limbs of the old cottonwood scraped against the side of the building, making his skin crawl.

He reached for the doorknob and realized it was sticky and wet with… The door swung open. He stared down at his hand in the dim light. Blood.

His gaze shot up at a sound. Jolene stood just inside

the door. Her face was distorted in fear, her mouth open. She was saying something but the wind was stealing her words before they reached him. Or maybe he didn't hear what she was saying because he was too busy staring at the butcher knife clutched in her hands, the blood dripping from the tip onto the hardwood floor at the feet.

Her mouth opened but he never heard her yell.

The blow came out of the darkness. Something hard and cold struck his temple. He reached, his fingers brushing fabric as he fell, a familiar face peering down just before the darkness closed in around him.

DULCIE WAITED ANXIOUSLY for something more to appear on the screen. She could hear the howl of wind and looked up to see tree branches whipping in the gale outside. Shadows flickered wildly. She could barely make out the dim light at the schoolhouse.

Russell must have reached the schoolhouse. That's why Jolene had quit typing the story. She glanced out the window toward the faint light glowing through the blackness.

She started to push away from the computer when words began to appear again.

You killed your own mother.

And now you have to kill yourself the same way you killed her. It's the only way your story will end.

Dulcie stared at the screen in horror. Jolene wasn't the one writing this. She shot up out of the chair and ran to the door, praying she wasn't too late.

Chapter Fourteen

"Russell! Russell!" The wind tore away her words and lashed her hair around her face as Dulcie ran up the road toward the schoolhouse. Lightning flickered on the horizon. A soft boom sounded like gunfire in the distance.

Up the road she could see the dim light in the building. A shadow moved in front of it, making her catch her breath. Jolene? Or Russell?

The first cold drops of rain splattered on the dusty ground, pelting her as they began to fall harder. The rain mixed with her tears of fear as she topped the hill and, turning into the school yard, came up short.

The door into the schoolhouse stood wide-open.

"Russell?" She mounted the steps cautiously. "Russell?" No answer and yet she'd just seen someone inside when she was coming up the hill.

She stepped through the small cloakroom with its hooks and shelves for coats and boots. As she rounded the corner, she saw her sister.

Jolene stood at the front of the classroom, her back to the wall. A large, bloody knife on the floor at her feet. Her sister didn't seem to hear her come in.

Oh, God, where was Russell? "Jolene?" Dulcie said cautiously.

"Run!" Jolene yelled. "Run, she has a—"

Gun. Dulcie saw the gun before Jolene got the word out.

Ronda Carpenter stepped out from behind the door to the supply room, holding a semiautomatic in both hands, the barrel pointed at Dulcie's chest. Her face was twisted into a nasty sneer and the left side of her blouse was soaked with what looked like blood.

A trail of blood drops led from Ronda to the computer on the side of the classroom. Next to the chair was a small pool of blood where Ronda had apparently been sitting. Sitting typing the murder story, Dulcie realized.

"Close the door and lock it," Ronda ordered.

"Where's Russell?" Dulcie asked, her voice cracking as she closed the door and pretended to lock it. She was soaked to the skin and shivering, terrified for the man.

"Now go over and stand by your sister," Ronda ordered.

Dulcie met Jolene's terrified gaze and read more than fear in it. "Where is Russell?" she asked, this time of Jolene.

Jolene looked as if she were in shock. "I'm starting to remember," she whispered. "It's my fault. I wished our mother dead. I—"

"That's right," Ronda said. "You killed her."

"No, I loved her. I didn't want her killed."

"You told my son you wanted her dead!" Ronda cried. "You told my son. My beautiful boy."

Jolene was crying now. "I didn't mean it. I was angry at her for making me go with the rainmaker to live somewhere else. I knew things wouldn't be better there. I knew."

Dulcie thought she understood now. Nine-year-old Tinker Horton wanting to help his little friend, wanting to protect his pregnant mother because he thought his stepfather was having an affair with Laura. Wanting to spare Angel from trying to take care of a self-absorbed mother.

"Ben *was* having an affair with Laura," Dulcie said. "Was he going to leave you, and Tinker thought he could keep Ben from going and you from being hurt by killing Laura?"

Ronda laughed. "Ben hated Laura because she was encouraging me to leave him. I was the one leaving Ben—until he found out I was pregnant. He didn't give a damn about me, but he wanted his kid." Bitterness rimmed her voice. "Tinker thought Ben threw me down the stairs to get rid of the baby because he wanted to be with Laura. He'd seen Ben coming from Laura's house. He didn't know that Ben had gone over there to threaten Laura to stay away from me and quit putting fool ideas into my head."

"How could you stay with a man who threw you down a flight of stairs?" Dulcie asked.

Ronda shook her head, anger and bitterness burning in her eyes. "I threw *myself* down the stairs. I knew if I had that baby, I'd never be free of Ben. Laura was my best friend. She promised to help me leave him."

Dulcie felt her blood turn to ice. This woman was crazy. Or maybe worse, completely sane and evil. "But you *stayed* with him."

"He was blackmailing me! He knew Tinker killed Laura. He was going to the sheriff unless I stayed with him. He said I owed him a baby."

Mace. Mace had been the baby she owed Ben? "Why would you make a bargain like that?" Dulcie demanded, horrified. "You had to know that one day it would come out. That Jolene would remember..." The rest of her words died away as she realized that Ronda was the one who'd gotten Jolene back to Whitehorse.

RUSSELL CAME TO IN the dark to the sound of driving rain. At first he thought he must be dreaming, it had been so long since he'd heard rain like that.

His head ached and he felt confused. He touched his temple and came away with blood on his fingers. It took a moment for him to remember what had happened.

He sat up with a start, his head swimming. Dulcie! He'd left her at Jolene's house but, knowing her, she wouldn't have stayed there long. She would have come looking for him. She would have—

He shoved away the thought as he remembered Jolene standing in the schoolhouse, a bloody knife in her hand.

Rain pounded the tin roof overhead. He realized that he must be in the garden shed next to the schoolhouse because he'd seen the lawnmower and some garden tools in the flash of lightning.

Staggering to his feet, he tried the door, not surprised to find it locked from the outside. He felt around in the dark shed until he found a hoe and using it as a lever was able to force it between the shed door and the wall.

The cheap latch on the shed door gave with a snap. Still holding the hoe, Russell listened but could hear nothing except the storm. He'd been so wrong about who killed Laura Beaumont, he thought, as he shoved open the shed door and looked out into the rain.

He moved quickly, the hoe in both hands like a bat in case he ran into the person who'd hit him. But there was no one outside the shed nor along the side of the schoolhouse. He reached the front, saw that the door stood open, just as before.

Only this time, he was ready in case Tinker Horton was lying in wait for him.

"WHY DID I STAY WITH BEN? Tinker was my baby," Ronda said, choking on tears. "I would do anything to protect Tinker—"

They all froze at the sound of a key in the schoolhouse lock. Dulcie realized that whoever was coming in didn't realize that she hadn't locked the door.

Ronda smiled as Tinker came in, soaked from the rain. He didn't bother to close the door, seeming in a hurry. "I took care of it for you, Mama," he said, then saw his mother's bloody blouse and staggered back. "Oh, no. What happened?"

"It's okay, baby. It's just a flesh wound," Ronda said. "I'm fine. *We're* fine. But there are a couple more things you're going to have to take care of for me, sweetheart."

Tinker seemed to see Dulcie and Jolene then. His eyes widened and he began to shake his head as he saw the bloody knife on the floor.

"Now don't get queasy on me, Tinker. Once we clean this up, it will be over," Ronda said soothingly. "No one will ever know what you did."

"Tinker didn't kill Laura," Jolene said.

Ronda's gaze narrowed. "Ben saw him with the knife. He had blood all over him. He was crying. He—"

"I startled the killer," Jolene said, her eyes glazed, her voice sounding strange, as if she were back there in that room that night. "The killer dropped the knife. Tinker had followed me to the house. I saw him as I ran out. He must have picked up the knife." Her gaze seemed to clear. "Tinker didn't kill Laura." She looked at the rodeo cowboy. "You didn't kill her."

"Now don't you go trying to confuse my boy," Ronda said. "He knows what he did and he—"

Dulcie saw Jolene swing her gaze to Ronda. "*You* killed her, Ronda. I *saw* you. I heard what you were saying. You'd found out she was running off with the rainmaker. She'd lied about helping you when you left Ben. In fact, she's the one who told Ben you were pregnant, wasn't she?"

"You let your son believe all these years that he—"

"Shut up!" Ronda snapped, cutting Dulcie off. "Don't listen to her, Tinker. She's the one who told you she wanted her mother dead, remember? She's the one who's to blame for this."

Dulcie caught movement out of the corner of her eye. Russell had entered the schoolhouse and was sneaking along the cloakroom wall behind Tinker and his mother. Dulcie's heart soared, then came crashing down. Ronda had a gun. She had to warn him. Or at least distract Ronda.

"Once we take care of things," Ronda was saying, "I can leave Ben for good, just like you've always wanted me to do, Tinker."

"You didn't stay with Ben because of Tinker," Dulcie said. "Ben must know the truth. That's why you stayed with him. He *was* blackmailing you, but not about Tinker."

Tinker suddenly went pale. "No, tell me that isn't why you had me…" His voice broke and Dulcie felt as if she might be sick.

"Ben was a bastard," Ronda said to her son. "You did the world a favor." She glanced down at her bleeding side. "Look what your precious Angel did to me. She tried to kill me because of you."

"She's lying, Tinker," Jolene said, sounding more

calm than Dulcie right now. "Your mother took the knife from me and stabbed herself in the side."

"That's a lie," Ronda snapped, then laughed. "Why would I stab myself?"

"She has a gun," Jolene said. "Would I stab a woman holding a gun? She is going to blame all of this on you, Tinker. She's going to let you take the fall for all of it."

Tinker looked to his mother. Like Dulcie, he must have seen Ronda's hand holding the gun waver as she considered turning it on her son.

Russell had moved closer, his eyes on Dulcie. She knew it was now or never. She looked down at the knife on the floor, then up at Russell. He nodded.

Things got crazy after that. Dulcie shoved her sister and kicked out at the knife. She heard it clatter across the old wooden floor toward Russell as she threw her sister and herself behind Jolene's large desk.

The gunshot boomed in the small school. Behind Dulcie, the blackboard shattered, raining down onto the floor beside them. A second shot followed and a third on its heels.

Dulcie was on her feet, terrified what she would see when she rose from the floor.

Over the sound of pounding rain, she saw Russell standing over the bodies of Tinker Horton and his mother. Tinker still had the gun that he'd taken from his mother in his hand. Ronda lay on the floor next to the computer, the words she'd typed still visible across the room.

She was holding her chest where her son had shot her before taking his own life. Her eyes were wide with surprise, even in death. Just as Laura Beaumont's had been.

Epilogue

Dulcie didn't hear Kate Corbett approach. It wasn't until she sat down next to her in the large Trails West Ranch living room that she stirred from her thoughts.

"Beautiful view, isn't it?" Kate said. "I never tire of sitting here. But it must be very different from Chicago and what you're used to."

Dulcie knew Kate hadn't joined her to talk about the view. "I was just thinking about Russell."

"I know," Kate said. "He's in love with you. But your life is in Chicago, isn't it?"

"It used to be," Dulcie said.

"He'll go back with you, if it's what you want," Kate said. "I know Russell. He'd do anything for you."

Dulcie knew he would. She'd fought him when he'd tried to protect her, believing she had to hang on to her independence. But something had changed since the night at the schoolhouse. It gave her nightmares to think how Tinker could have just as easily wrenched the gun from his mother's hand and turned it on Russell instead of his mother and himself.

A brush with death changed people. It had changed her. Just as this man and this land had changed her.

"I wouldn't ask Russell to go back to Chicago with

me," she said. "I know how much he loves ranching with his father. It isn't just the ranch. His family is here."

Kate rose to her feet. "There are worse things than him leaving his family and the ranch. I couldn't bear to see his heart broken. I know Russell. He doesn't love easily. There won't ever be anyone else but you. Let him go with you. If you love him."

Left alone with only the view of the Montana prairie and the Little Rockies in the distance, Dulcie thought about Russell, her feelings for him and what was waiting for her back in Chicago. Then seeing the time, she hurried to her car.

On the drive into town, she found herself reliving the night at the schoolhouse. In a flash of lightning, she'd seen Russell rush to her, drag her into his arms and lead her and Jolene outside. Life and death. Only a flash of lightning between them.

Russell had kept saying her name, over and over, as he held her. Water ran from the brim of his hat and the soft, dark strands of hair at the nape of his neck. He blinked back the rain, his blue eyes alight with the storm and her.

"I love you!" he'd yelled over the pounding rain. "I love you, Dulcie Hughes!"

He'd held her tight, rain and the tears running down her face in the darkness. She had turned her face up to the rain, letting her tears finally come. Around her lightning flashed, thunder boomed and she'd cried for the mother she never knew and for her sister, the blessing, she'd almost lost.

Laura Beaumont had lost herself here. Her youngest daughter had found herself, Dulcie thought. And found a sister she'd never known she had.

Would she ever be able to forgive her grandparents?

In time. She told herself that they had known she would find Jolene. And save her? Or was that just her way of dealing with it, believing there'd been a plan bigger than herself?

She knew they had blamed themselves until their dying days for leaving Angel. For leaving Laura.

But Angel had survived it. She smiled at the thought of her sister, Jolene. A strong woman like herself. Jolene would be fine. In time.

Speaking of Jolene, Dulcie thought. Her sister would be waiting for her at Northern Lights.

JOLENE LOOKED UP AS HER sister came into the restaurant. Her sister. She'd always wanted siblings. She smiled and rose to give her a hug. They held each other for a long moment.

"I hope you're hungry," Jolene said. "Laci insisted on cooking us something special for lunch."

Dulcie laughed. "I'm starved, but then I always am."

Jolene studied her. "How are you?"

"Better. How about you?"

Jolene nodded. "I feel lighter." She laughed. "I took your advice. I'm seeing a psychologist. Talking about it helps."

She understood why she'd hidden her truth for so long and so deep. She'd believed she'd caused her mother's death because of one weak moment on the creek that night when she'd wished her mother gone.

"I just feel bad about Tinker. Maybe if I had remembered sooner…"

"Don't do that to yourself," Dulcie said. "Ben knew the kind of woman he was living with. How is Mace, though?"

"The Whitehorse Sewing Circle is finding him a home," Jolene said. "Pearl assured me that they would find him a good one and make sure he was all right."

"Here, I want you to have this." Dulcie pulled some papers from her shoulder bag and slid them across the table.

"Dulcie—"

"It's the money from the property and half of the estate our grandparents left us."

"Dulcie, no. They left that to you."

Her sister shook her head, smiling. "No, you see that's the thing I figured out. Why they didn't tell me about you, about the Montana property, about our mother. I think they felt their hands were tied, but they knew me. They knew I wouldn't give up until I got to the bottom of it. Until I found my sister and made things right."

Jolene looked down at the check, then back up at her sister. "It's so much."

"Enough so that you never have to work again."

Jolene shook her head. "I love teaching. I didn't get into it for the money, that's for sure," she added with a smile.

Dulcie reached across the table and took her hand. "I'd hoped you'd say that. You're a great teacher."

Laci appeared then with a huge tray. "I made you samplers of all my favorites."

They dug in, complimenting each dish and thanking Laci for her thoughtfulness.

After she was gone, Jolene asked her sister, "What about you? What will you do now?"

Dulcie shook her head, a faraway look in her eyes. "Russell has invited me to stay out at the ranch for a while."

"How are things with the two of you?"

"I've never met anyone like him."

"I'm sure he's never met anyone like you," Jolene said with a laugh. "I'm glad you're staying for a while. We have a lot of catching up to do."

Dulcie's gaze locked with hers. "You were always in my heart and no matter what the future holds I'm never going to be more than a phone call away."

IT HAD CLOUDED UP AGAIN by the time Dulcie drove back toward the ranch. As she passed the Whitehorse Cemetery, she slowed when she saw the rainmaker's truck parked beside the road.

She could make out his dark silhouette standing on the hill by Laura Beaumont's grave. She saw him put the small bouquet of flowers by the headstone and turn to leave. Stopping the car, she rolled down her window as she waited for him.

Finnegan Amherst saw her but there was no longer any malice in his expression, just grief. "Maybe now she can rest in peace. Maybe we all can."

"I'm sorry I misjudged you," she said as he started past her car.

He stopped and looked back at her. "You *do* look like your mother. She was a beautiful woman. But she wasn't strong. Not like you. She would have been proud of you and your sister…and sorry." He nodded, tears shining in his dark eyes.

With a tip of his floppy black hat, he walked to his pickup and climbed in as large drops of rain began to fall.

Dulcie sat, thinking about her mother. Had the rainmaker been the love of her life? Or had it been Dulcie and Angel's father? Or would Laura Beaumont have spent her life looking for that one man who would love her the way she so desperately needed to be loved?

The way Russell loved her, Dulcie thought.

The rainmaker's pickup engine started, rumbling roughly, and he drove away, the metal pipes in the back of his truck clinking softly to the sound of the rain.

RUSSELL SAW DULCIE drive up and went out on the porch. She'd been quiet all morning and when he saw her face he knew she'd made a decision.

She stepped out of the car and stood, her face turned up to the rain. He'd never seen a more beautiful woman, never loved her more than he did at that moment. He had to let her go. He'd known that from the start. Just as he knew he would go with her—if she let him.

She must have sensed him standing there because she looked in his direction, a big smile spreading across her face. "I love you!" she called through the pouring rain. "I love you, Russell Corbett."

He realized it was the first time she'd said it. He felt his heart take off at a gallop. "I love you, Dulcie," he called back.

"Marry me and build me a house over there on that hillside."

He met her gaze and was off that porch in a heartbeat, lifting her off her feet to whirl her around as the rain fell, beading in her lashes and running down her face. And they were laughing and he was telling her how much he loved her and then his mouth was on hers and slowly he was lowering her to the ground.

As he pulled back, both of them soaked to the skin, he had to ask, "Are you sure, Dulcie? This is no Chicago."

She laughed. "No, Russ, it's not. But this is where our children will grow up and, if we're lucky, our grandchildren. This is where my heart is."

* * * * *

*Bailey Lockhart claims she doesn't need
a bodyguard. Thankfully Parker McKenna
doesn't listen and is there to protect her when
a mysterious stalker comes calling....
Find out what happens next in* GI COWBOY
*by Delores Fossen, available April 2011
from Harlequin Intrigue.*

With his gun aimed and ready, Parker inched inside Bailey's office. His gaze whipped to all the corners. Then to her desk that had been tipped onto its side. Papers and her laptop were now in a heap on the floor.

Two chairs had also been overturned, and the room had generally been trashed. But what was missing was the person who'd done all of this.

Parker walked farther into the room, toward a storage closet.

Also vandalized.

The small adjoining bathroom hadn't escaped harm, either. Someone had poured out the liquid soap. And then he spotted the open window on the far wall. When he got closer, he saw the ladder propped up against the side of the building. Probably the point of entry and escape.

He glanced back at Bailey to let her know the place was clear, that her stalker was likely long gone, but the look on her face had Parker walking toward her. There was no color left in her cheeks, and her blue eyes were wide with shock. She was breathing way too hard and fast, and he didn't want to risk her hyperventilating.

Parker caught on to her and pulled her back into the hall. But she maneuvered herself out of his grip and returned to her office. She was still visibly upset, but he could see the initial shock had worn off.

Bailey stood there, her back to him, her upper body moving with her still-heavy breath. She was literally the only spot of order in the room. If it hadn't been for the mess around her, she would have looked ready for a staff meeting in her perfectly fitted turquoise top and gray pants. There wasn't a strand of her dark blond shoulder-length hair out of place.

"You still think you don't need a bodyguard?" Parker asked.

Yeah, it wasn't a nice question, but he couldn't play nice here with Bailey and her safety. He needed her to understand how the slashed tires and hang-up calls could escalate.

And now she was looking at proof of that escalation.

She didn't acknowledge his question. Instead, she stooped down and reached for a framed photo.

"Don't touch anything," Parker warned. "The sheriff will probably want to process the scene for prints or other evidence."

Her hand froze, and Parker saw then that it was a picture of Bailey, her mother and her two siblings. The glass and frame had both been shattered.

Parker kept an eye on her and called Sheriff Bernard Hale. Freedom's police department wasn't exactly large or cutting edge, but he'd already had several discussions with Sheriff Hale and knew the man would do his best to find something, anything, that would help identify the person who was trying to make Bailey's life a living hell.

"The sheriff's coming out now," Parker informed her after he made the call. He slipped his phone back in his pocket, caught her arm again and took her out of the room. "Is there a way for you to get in touch with your staff and students so you can tell them not to come in today?"

Well, that put the color back in her cheeks. "That won't be necessary. It's obvious the stalker's not here. It's also obvious that his venom is aimed only at me."

"For now," Parker mumbled. "But it could get worse."

"I don't want to close Cradles to Crayons," she snapped. "I'll add security. There's a system already wired in, but we don't normally use it. We will now. And maybe I can hire you to watch the place."

Parker gave her a flat look. "I already have a job."

"That's debatable."

* * * * *

How will these two stand to be around each other without their undeniable attraction getting in the way? Find out in GI COWBOY *by* USA TODAY *bestselling author Delores Fossen, available April 2011 from Harlequin Intrigue.*

Spread the joy of love and romance!

Smokin' Six Shooter is a heart-pounding story of a city girl who travels to Montana to claim her secret inheritance. But what she doesn't expect is to unearth a long-forgotten murder mystery and fall in love with the handsome rancher who may have a few secrets of his own....

This is a story you can share with friends, family, book club members or anyone you think would enjoy a suspenseful, romantic read!

Here are some ideas for sharing books:

◆ Give to your sister, daughter, granddaughter, mother, friends or coworkers
◆ Host your own book club
◆ Share the books with members of your community, church group or PTA
◆ Share them at your community center, retirement home or hospital to brighten someone's day

OR

◆ Feel free to leave them for others to enjoy on an airplane, in a coffee shop, at the Laundromat, doctor's or dentist's office, hairdresser, spa or vacation spot

Please tell us about your experience reading and sharing these books at
www.tellharlequin.com.